HIGH JINKS

AT THE

HIGH HILL

HOTEL

Praise for Horatio BLOOM

'This enchantingly woven story ensnares you from the very first page to the last, with a cast of characters you really care about. A magnificent energetic work of high art from a new author blazing their way in the world of fiction. What an amazing debut from author Charles Linton.'

Included in Error

'I've never read the book you hold in your hands, but the law of averages say it should be mediocre.'

Random Person on the Street

'He's the salt of the Earth. Why yes, he did pay me to say that. Is that wrong?'

Bribed Simpleton

'Well, that's a few hours of my life I won't be getting back again.'

Horatio BLOOM's Editor

'He's a shifty looking person him, I mean who dresses like that on a sunny day, it's just not right.'

Sunbathing Expert

'A ludicrous plot with unbelievable characters and pacing that all but guarantees the reader will suffer from narcolepsy.'

The Little Didwob Gazette

Also by this most distinguished Author

Knobbly Knees and Other Manly Attributes*

Homes With Domes and Garden Gnomes**

Chronic Coughs of the Rich and Famous***

Notable Sneezes of the Famous and Rich****

Rogues in Brogues - A History of Fearsome Footwear
and the Espadrilles of Evil*****

*
**
***
****
***** Please do not attempt to search for any of these titles at your local bookstore, technically none of these have been written yet. Sorry, there are only so many hours in the day...

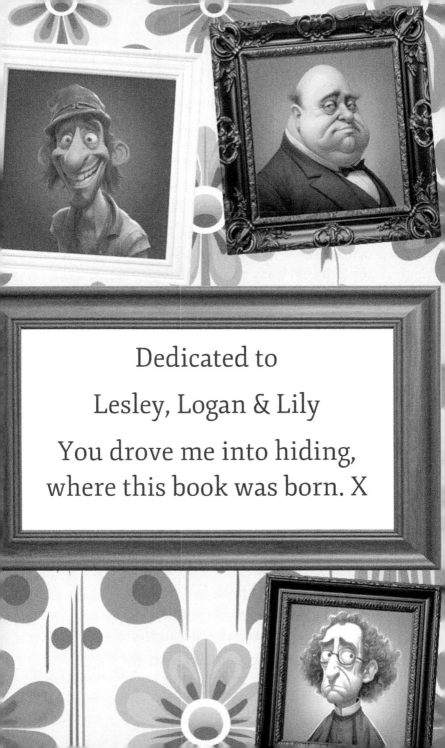

Dedicated to

Lesley, Logan & Lily

You drove me into hiding, where this book was born. X

For continued disappointment please following at

 www.horatiobloom.com ✗ @Horatio_BLOOM

Fonts

Fjord by Viktoriya Grabowska

Manun by AmruID

Yeasty Flavors by Niskala Huruf

Curely by Konstantine Studio

Seuss by 538Fonts

All courtesy of **FontSpace**.

HIGH JINKS AT THE HIGH HILL HOTEL

Horatio BLOOM

Quantum
Affiliation

Author's Note

You do not know me, which is just the way I like it. I shall divulge this however, I am a collector of tales. Tall tales, wide tales, tales about whales or space snails and the tale I will now regale - you will enjoy immensely. If not then we have a small problem, mostly in your general direction, so I shall make it clear in the clearest legalese as possible - there is no money back and any time invested in this little venture was yours to waste. Now, I am sure we can dispense with these little trifles, as you are moments away from reading the story and I am sure your little heart will soon be beating like a drum and your eyes will simply bulge with amazement. I should add that the names may, or may not, have been changed to protect the innocent. As startling as this may seem, this is a true story. Or is it? Did I just make that up? Sometimes I cannot remember myself. Or even what I had for breakfast this morning. It may have been toast, as I did spot some crumbs on my scarf, but those could have been there from yesterday, or yesteryear. Anyway, I find myself babbling and if babbling is of special interest to you, then you have hit the jackpot. Read on...

Horatio BLOOM

Prologue

The Police Sergeant was not sure if it was rainwater, or a bead of sweat generated by the topsy-turvy scenes that had played out since his arrival. He could feel it zigging and zagging as it meandered along his furrowed brow. He tried to beat it out of the way with his eyebrows. To the casual observer, and there were many in the room, it looked as if the poor man was in the early throes of a seizure, such was their furious twitching.

The mad fluttering of these hairy pinball flippers was all for nought as the trickle, growing in greater momentum, as well as size, ran down to the end of his bulbous red nose. And stopped.

He tried his best to ignore it, but by squinted his eyes hard, which he was, he could see the translucent droplet sitting there, mocking him.

Concern for the wellbeing of the Sergeant had grown within the room, his list of ailments now including sudden bursts of cross-eyed fever.

His thoughts were on more pressing matters. He needed to restore some form of order, gain a measure of control, be...

commanding. He was an officer of the law, even if he was standing here in nothing but sodden underwear.

The accursed droplet finally succumbed to the forces of gravity and plummeted from his nose onto the floor with a tiny splash. For some reason its slow-motion descent annoyed him, as did the fact that everyone in the room seemed to be fixated upon its fate and watched its demise intently.

He was now feeling the early onset of a headache. It was pulling and tingling at the edges of his temple. The corner of his eye was also beginning to pulse, although that may have had more to do with the recent bout of eyeball gymnastics recently performed.

On this dark and stormy night, he had the great misfortune to have stumbled into the calamitous chaos of this gothic madhouse. Murder, theft, the walking dead, ghosts, and a stench from the bowels of Hell itself. Those only happened to be the things of which he was unfortunately aware. He could not pretend he fully understood just what had taken place this day. He knew one thing however, a shining certainty in this fog of confusion, and that was if he stood here for much longer something else ludicrous would surely unfold.

With the drip now having bored its audience of the hotel's weird workers and ridiculous residents, he could feel their eyes on him once again. They were looking to him for advice and guidance. There had been some high jinks here tonight, that was for certain. The paperwork for all this was going to be epic.

'I've made ma decision,' he growled. He felt another pool of water gathering on the end of his nose. Forget the headache, he was going to have a corker of a cold soon.

'Until backup arrives, I'm placing every single one o' ye... under arrest!'

Chapter 1

Perry could tell it was a dream. His Uncle Hugo's head was about ten times bigger than normal, and for the record, *'normal'* was unusually large. Also, his trademark waddle was nowhere to be seen. He was now bouncing around like a spaceman on the moon, step by floating step.

'**I want you OUT. OUT of my hotel. OUT now,**' he squeaked in a surprisingly falsetto voice.

'Please no, have mercy,' came a plea.

Perry turned, it was his father, Erstwhile. He was on his knees begging. In fact, they were all on their knees in a line. Perry and his parents, all at the whim of their demented, inflated relative.

'**You have to GO,**' came the high-pitched reply, '**I want you OUT.**'

'Please Uncle, don't do this,' Perry heard himself cry. 'This is our home, we have nowhere else to go, you don't have the right.'

'**Oh, but I do,**' mocked his buoyant uncle who laughed and turned his giant grotesque balloon head towards him. '**I got rid of your mother didn't I,**' from behind his back he produced a large sharp glinting hat pin.

Perry whipped his head around to look at his mother, still kneeling next to him. To his horror she was now a balloon person too. Perry tried to do something, anything, but light as a feather as his uncle seemed to be, he was a dead weight, his arms and legs heavy as lead. He was powerless.

Perry was forced to watch as Uncle Hugo drifted over to his mother and pricked her with the pin.

A loud undignified farting noise erupted and echoed throughout the hotel reception, where Perry realised, they were all assembled. His mother zoomed off. She propelled across the hall, bouncing off one wall and another, the ceiling and then the floor. A bag of hot air rapidly deflating as she fluttered around madly. Then, in a last rasping gush of wind, she rocketed out of the open hotel door that magically slammed closed behind her.

'**Now it's your turn Brother,**' cheered Uncle Hugo, who was bouncing on the spot, as if on an inflatable castle. He stopped, suspended mid air, hovering in all his menacing glory.

'**It's been fun, but all good things must come to an end.**' A lightning quick jab followed to the arm of his brother.

'No, Dad, are you okay? Dad...,' shouted Perry.

His father's demise was slightly more dignified than that of his mother. He was slowly deflating, his features melting as his form collapsed in on itself. It crumpled up until there was nothing left, but a mere cardboard cut out of him lying on the floor.

'Please, please don't, this has been our home forever,' implored Perry.

'I... DON'T... CARE,' squeaked his uncle with a devilish laugh. He sprang around the room, recoiling off objects at unfathomable angles. The hat pin he had been slashing back and forth had now grown and was the size of a dagger.

'It's time for you to go, it's time for you to go,' he sang tunelessly. He had now stopped flying around and was levitating above the floor, hanging there in front of Perry. His massive face comically blown out of all proportion.

As frightening a sight as this was, Perry could not help but notice something from the corner of his eye. As he focussed, he could see the faint image of an elderly gentleman, a pleasant looking fellow, standing at the foot of the reception stairs. Perry was going to cry to him for help but knew none would be forthcoming, this was a dream after all.

It did give Perry an idea, he needed to buy some time. He breathed in deeply and blew with all his might in the direction of his blimp of an uncle. He did not expect it to work, so was heartened when his uncle started to spin backwards wildly out of control into the corner of the room.

Perry brought his attention back to the shimmering old man. He was dressed in a pair of blue medieval looking robes, the sleeves of which were covered in ornate swirling designs of silver thread. It was what lay atop his head that Perry focussed on. He was wearing a crown, a simple golden ringlet, but front and centre sat the largest red ruby Perry had ever seen. It was beautiful.

Perry also now noticed that around the man's neck sat a large livery collar of thick silver chain, embedded with a multitude of sapphires. It was enchanting.

In his aged hands he gripped a sceptre of considerable size, golden like the crown, inlaid with the greenest of emeralds. It was remarkable.

'*Find me,*' the ghostly figure mouthed.

'I'm sorry, what?' Perry could not make sense of his plea.

'*Find me,*' he repeated.

The almost forgotten Uncle Hugo, his deadly hat pin now morphed to sword length, was slowly approaching the distracted Perry.

'*Find me,*' the phantom like King whispered. '*Find me.*'

There was a glint from the crown which shone down on Perry, blinding his eyes. The sheer amount of light now radiating from the golden crown was tremendous. Perry's eyes were watering, the light was all encompassing. Everything was dissolving into a golden haze...

The one unmistakeable, undeniable truth about the High Hill Hotel was the fact it was a hotel, which sat upon an exceedingly High Hill. It was this proximity to the heavens, Perry believed, which caused the morning sunlight to be more... unusually aggressive.

At this very moment, the intrusive and pugnacious sunshine had managed to find a small gap between the curtains and was streaming in. It was slapping him in the face, plucking at his nostril hairs and shouting forcibly in his ear to wake up. To put aside any more thoughts of dreams and face the day. Perry put up a brave fight, but the cascading sunbeams were winning, and he was forced to open his heavy eyes and accept defeat.

'I'll find you; I'll find you,' Perry slurred, his mouth dry. He sat up and began to swing out of bed. 'I'll find you,' he muttered still half asleep. With a foggy brain, and still entangled in the bed clothes, all he quickly found was the bedroom floor, with a mighty crashing thud.

'**Ow...**'

Horatio BLOOM here; between you and myself, I believe this boy has been eating far too much cheese before bed. How else can you account for such a dream, or was it a nightmare? A lesson to all of you, when indulging in a nighttime snack. That said, as a child, I once ate an entire wheel of Edam before drifting off to sleep. It was a dream of epic proportions. It was only the one night for everyone else, but for me that dream lasted an entire year. I put that time to good use and when I awoke the next day — from my forever slumber — my parents were quite impressed at the breakfast table by the fact I could suddenly speak flawless Mandarin, play the moonlight sonata on the steel drums and was a competent taxidermist.

Chapter 2

Perry lay face down on the fluffy, albeit messy, floor of his bedroom. All was silent. All was still. He was trying to find the willpower to roust himself fully awake. He managed to meekly shake his legs, finally casting aside his bonds, and liberating himself from the sheets.

'Yay,' came a muffled cheer. There then followed a muted, 'happy days, it's the weekend.'

This provided him with enough enthusiasm to roll over onto his back, where he then performed a half-hearted fist pump. The bright cuddly joy of not having to go to school quickly dimmed however, after he reminded himself, he had work instead.

The hotel, just as he had, was now waking from its beauty sleep. It was reopening its briefly closed doors to the public today. Soon guests would be checking in and things around here would finally be getting back to normal.

'Normal,' he tutted, 'now that's a joke!'

As was his want, Uncle Hugo would always shut down the hotel in what he referred to as the off season. There was no real need of course and his father had tried to talk him out of it many times, but Uncle Hugo would not hear of it. The fact was, despite knowing nothing about running a hotel, even after all the years of supposedly operating one, he simply would not leave it in the hands of others. More to the point, Uncle Hugo would never forego his travels. He loved nothing better than to go gallivanting around the world.

At the very thought of his oafish uncle, Perry could feel the tears smarting at the corners of his eyes, so he decided to roll over until he was face down on the carpet again. Everything was his uncle's fault. Well, perhaps that wasn't entirely true, but by his reckoning a good 99% of it was.

The fact was Perry's mother had gone, left, over three days ago now. Off to spend a week with a friend after his parents' last barn stormer of an argument. One of many. They were now happening so often they blurred into each other. But Perry wasn't stupid, these spats were not just becoming too frequent, they were also becoming too intense and bitter. The last one had scared him.

'We have to get out of here Erstwhile,' his mother pleaded.

'It's the family business,' his father countered.

'No,' she hissed, 'it's your brother's business, this is Hugo's hotel, and we forever live in his shadow. He treats you and Perry like servants, and I'm not standing for it anymore...'

His mother wanted them to leave. Perry could not believe it. He began to feel the tears welling up again. He did not want to leave, and he knew his dad felt the same, but if they did not... could his parents really split up?

Perry could understand why his mother was angry. Uncle Hugo was a beast of a man. On his absolute best days, he treated his staff poorly and his family even worse.

As some form of cosmic joke his father and uncle were identical twins, yet they could not have been more different. Perry's dad was kind, considerate, good humoured and hard working; his only fault was that he let his older brother walk all over him. Uncle Hugo meanwhile was petty, cruel, abusive, and lazy. He made his brother run the hotel while he pottered around finding things to complain about. Any clever idea his brother produced was suddenly his own and any failure on his part was soon delegated down to his younger sibling.

As much as Perry hated to admit it, his mother was correct. It was a miracle they had lasted as a family for as long as they had. It also looked like she was going to get her wish. It may have been the only home that both he and his father had ever known, but it was coming to end, whether they liked it or not.

The prostate Perry punched the soft floor, and again for good measure. Any chance of talking his mother round was going to be pointless now, certainly after what he had recently uncovered. The paperwork that had been sitting there on his uncle's study table. He had either forgotten to hide it or just did not care anymore. He was planning to sell the hotel. A hotel that had been in the Bumbler family for centuries, and there was nothing they would be able to do about it.

For the last few days Perry felt as if he had been carrying the weight of the world on his shoulders. He had not told his father, how could he, the news would break him. Perry kept trying to convince himself that it would be for the best, maybe it could all work out. He wanted to have both parents together a lot more than he wanted to stay under this gothic roof.

Perry, from where he did not know, finally found the strength, to drag and pull himself over to his full-length mirror. He looked up and stared into it, feeling sorry for himself. Despite having been face down on the floor, for what felt like the best part of the morning, the first order of the day was to wipe away the drool from the corner of his mouth. It was reaching around his jaw like a snail's trail.

He also could not fail to detect the slight dark circles beneath his eyes. Recent events had taken their toll. He had been struggling to sleep of late, although last night had been a rare exception, as had the dream.

'Wow, I had a dream, a weird dream,' he said aloud, vaguely recalling something. 'It was... crazy, it was crazy and...,' Perry concentrated hard, how could he forget the dream? That dream that was quickly slipping away. He had to think, fast. What was so important about it? There was something he had to remember before it faded away, forever. He looked at himself in the mirror again.

'C'mon big guy, think.'

He secretly liked to call himself that, despite being the second shortest person in his class. Well, that was his opinion anyway, it happened to be a remarkably close contest between himself and Cheryl Plankton. She did wear a pair of huge, ungainly orthopaedic shoes however, which in his view gave her an unfair height advantage.

'YES,' he shouted when it finally came to him. His idiotic balloon uncle, and that strange ghostly looking king, bedecked in beautiful regalia. What was it he had been asking again?

Find me, his brain eventually filled in the blank. *Find me.* What could it possibly mean?

The sudden realisation of what the dream was telling him, hit Perry like a punch to the stomach. He refused to believe it. Pure ridiculousness. Farcical beyond words. The odds alone would be astronomical. But as crazy as it sounded, it was a chance none the less. Realistically, this could be his only solution.

Perry hauled himself to his feet and in a burst of energy began dressing, throwing on anything that came to hand. He needed to run all this past Malaika. Not only was she his best friend, but right now she might be his only hope. She could at times behave in a manner that suggested she was as mad as a box of frogs, but with this problem, he knew there was no one better equipped. She also would not flatter him, lie to him, or give him false hope either.

If he was to save his parents' marriage and secure the future of the hotel, then his crazy dream plan needed her, she was crucial to the entire thing.

Horatio BLOOM again; that reminds me of another instance when I had a dream. What I can reveal was that the resulting fantastical slumber formed the plot of a bestselling, award winning, novel that I wrote. No, before you ask, I am afraid it is not the one you hold in your hands.

Chapter 3

Perry did the mental calculations quickly in his head. His teacher would have been impressed and not once did he have to stick out his tongue to alleviate brain cramp. He reasoned that as he was not due to start the first of his new shifts until lunch time, if he were to quickly leave the hotel right now, he could get down to the village and back, with just enough time to spare.

'Oh mirror, mirror standing there, what's the score for what I wear,' said Perry to his reflection. Even he was quite unprepared for what he saw. It was as if someone had dressed themselves on a dare - in the dark - in a cramped and flimsy tent - during a hurricane. It was far from being socially acceptable, but in his ill-informed opinion, it mustered up an artistic dash of flair and elegance that he foolishly believed could be pulled off.

His dishevelled hair meanwhile looked like a bird was currently nesting in it, but that was normal. It always looked like that, even five minutes after a haircut. He also promised himself that upon his return he would treat himself, and therefore everyone else, to a rare shower and...

'**Crumbs**,' Perry wailed, how could he have forgotten?

Hanging there, on the side of his wardrobe was the new uniform his uncle had brought back from his recent travels. When Perry was last down in the village, he had completed some online research, which revealed it to be a form of 'Bellhop' attire. No doubt, in another hotel, his uncle had witnessed some poor unfortunate wear one and instantly thought it would work well over here. That or he had just found yet another torture device to make Perry's life insufferable.

After much thought and deliberation Perry had decided to give his uncle the rare benefit of the doubt. Unfortunately, when it came to fashion his uncle often seemed quite detached from reality. He would continually wear a succession of outlandish outfits that just boggled the mind and stung the senses. His uncle was perhaps just looking for a partner in crime.

The costume hung there in its overly starched slime green slumber, the trousers legs adorned with running golden stripes and the jacket handicapped with bulky golden buttons. To set off the entire experience was a jonty little hat. Perry prayed to any god that may have been listening, begging that none of his classmates would ever be at the hotel to see him wear this.

On grabbing his phone, he took a final lingering look at his cosy, comfortable bed and gave a heartfelt sigh. Quickly negated by the small shudder that erupted throughout him when he again spotted the new uniform. He rushed out of his room, the swinging door gently closing behind him.

Perry Bumbler now began the well trodden path from his room on the third floor down to the hotel's reception. This floor was only really used by family members or staff, which accounted for its dated and shabby appearance. All the other levels of the hotel were dedicated to the guests. As he strode down the corridor and took each winding turn, he marvelled at how deathly quiet everything was.

Silent, that was, aside from the gentle farting of a mouse. Only it was not a rodent's squeaky flatulence, it was his annoying shoes. No matter how long he had worn them they continued to cause him great embarrassment and all manner of psychological distress. The noise would come and go, there was no logic to their squeaky protest, their high-pitched taunting. It was just something he had to live with. He was not due a new pair of shoes for at least a couple of months yet.

SQUEAK... **SQUEAL**... **CHEEP**...

On they went, the noise getting louder and louder with ever accursed step he took. Just blank it out old bean, thought Perry to himself, you can do it. Just imagine you are in physics class, just blank it all out.

His thoughts turned to the hotel again as he remembered there was the slight possibility that a guest may have arrived late last night. If so, then the hotel was officially back in business quicker than expected, so no running, no carrying on. He had to be on his best behaviour.

Now, on the second floor, the guest rooms he breezed past would soon all start filling up. The staffing levels in the hotel would increase to cater for the demand. Before you knew it, the place would be animated with the day-to-day hustle and bustle. The sound of luggage banging against the walls in the ongoing struggle to get it up the stairs, on account of Uncle Hugo not installing the convenience of an elevator. The gentle buzz of muzak, intertwined with the background litany of conversation, compliments, and complaints. The stench of attempted cooking, the clattering of plates, the clinking of cutlery and the cries of even more complaints.

This was when the old building truly came alive, and despite his chores, Perry loved it. This hotel was in his blood just as much as it was in his father's, and he was now more determined than ever to save it. He could not allow his uncle to abandon this place to some soulless corporation.

As he walked on, his now non-squeaking shoes, sank into the freshly vacuumed plush carpet, its deep maroon complimenting the wallpaper. It was a vibrant horse and hound scene, where everyone looked bamboozled, searching for the sly old fox that was one step ahead and much too clever for the pursuing pack. This was all his fathers doing. He would always ensure the hotel had a good clean and spruce up whenever his uncle went a wandering. He knew how important it was to keep up appearances. If his penny-pinching uncle had his way, the entire hotel would have looked as grotty as the third floor.

Perry continued, past freshly painted doors and through the impressive high-ceilinged archways with their ornate cornices. He left in his wake a small display in the corner which proudly declared, to anyone who was interested, that some 150 years previously, Lord Smorgasbord Beaverbeard had not only visited the hotel, but as a bonus, on this very spot, had thrown up his lunch of curried parsnips in a goat's cheese crumble. The hotel it seemed carried a longstanding tradition of employing poor cooks. If they ever decided to formally recognise everyone who had been sick recently, then there would be no room left in the hotel for guests.

Soon Perry was down to the first floor and deep in thought about what he was going to say to Malaika - *daydreaming was another word for it* - and having raised his eyes from his shabby looking shoes he jumped back in shock. He was face to face with an ugly ogre of a man, eyes as black as night with wild, untamed hair...

In all fairness, I did warn that chap Beaverbeard, I was a bit of an innovator when it came to cooking. I did like to push the boundaries wherever possible back then. I would like to put on the record that I have never put gunpowder in a curry again after that reaction. Oh, and do not think I did not notice that little urchin of a boy flee his room earlier without even brushing his teeth. How very grim. HB

Chapter 4

'Oh, it's you Broadstroke,' wheezed Perry, clutching at his beating chest. 'I sometimes forget you like to jump out on the unexpected.'

The grand old hotel had been in the Bumbler family for generations, continually passed down to the eldest child as was the tradition. Despite having lived here all his days, no matter how many times he walked its halls and corridors, Perry's eyes were continually drawn towards the litany of paintings that dotted the walls.

A few were of the hotel itself, which if viewed in the correct order, made you realise just how much it had changed over the years, especially the missing North Tower. This had been accidentally burned to the ground by the ill-famed Chunder Bumbler, in his attempts at alchemy and his desire to turn lead into gold. He instead transformed part of a perfectly good building into ash, after leaving his Bunsen burner unattended.

The remaining artwork concerned a different topic. In a variety of different sizes, eclectic painting styles and gaudy frames, were the bizarre, quite often surprised looking faces of former Bumbler hotel owners.

Perry was currently standing before the huge oil painting of the infamous Broadstroke Bumbler. Long red untamed hair, thick tangled moustache, unkempt matted beard, all spilled from the portrait. Unless you had studied it previously, you almost had to search for the rictus grin, which sat beneath a bent, often broken nose. And those haunting eyes, they stared into your very soul, never failing to trigger a shiver down the spine. Of all the hotel's paintings, this had always been the one that captured Perry's attention the most. He had once questioned his father about his savage looking ancestor.

'He was a giant of a man by all accounts,' his dad explained. 'He took part in all manner of strongman competitions across the land. Moving great heavy rocks from A to B, for no apparent reason. Rolling cows up steep hills, whether they liked it or not.

Moving heavier and more enormous rocks from B to A. And who needs a horse, when you can pull a fully loaded cart with your teeth alone. You name it, if there was a wager on it, he would do it. In fact, he once held the record for the most ridiculous challenge ever. A challenge so ridiculous, no one could believe he did it, so they cancelled the record and quickly forgot all about it.'

'He looked so fierce,' replied a young Perry, looking up at the giant painting.

'There's a story that he once wrestled a bear.'

'Is that how he died?'

'Oh no, the story was he was winning the fight easily, but he was disqualified for tweaking the poor beast's nipples. No, old Broadstroke Bumbler met his end crushed in the horrid Highlands of Scotland, during a caber tossing competition. Very changeable weather in that part of the world Perry. One minute he was vigorously tossing it, a perfect end over end. Then, a surprise gust of wind and it was an imperfect end over end heading straight back towards him. As a mark of respect, they used that very caber to make his coffin. They also don't like to waste things in that part of the world.'

Being mindful of the time Perry continued down the corridor, passing one of the smaller art works on display. This humble water colour was the impression of Hallelujah Bumbler. He was a thin lipped, sour looking man, as complete an opposite of Broadstroke Bumbler as you could hope to find, especially in the flowing locks department. Completely bald, save from a few tufts of scraggly hair above the ears which were hanging on for dear life. They had obviously not received the memo to abandon ship. He wore a pair of small, but thick, gold spectacles and was seated behind a table full of dusty looking scrolls and manuscripts.

Hallelujah had been a bitter man who had yearned to be a writer, rather than a hotel owner. A collection of his unpublished books and plays still resided in the hotel library. Perry attempted to read one of them once, a peculiar tale of a hermit living in a cave, high in the mountains. He feasted on toenails, drank his own bathwater and his best friend was a lettuce, called Minky. Understandably Perry had given up after a few pages.

It was clearly obvious that Hallelujah would never have achieved literary success and sadly there was no happy ending for him either. A premature exit, from an infected paper cut, closed the chapter on his disappointing life.

Perry was now on the home strait, passing all the others honoured to have their likeness on display. Well, likeness was perhaps pushing things. Flotsam Bumbler, thanks to cubism, was nought but a blue box with three eyes. A pair of full lips sat where his nose should have been and an eyebrow where his mouth was missing. Ticklewick Bumbler, a fan of surrealism, had a bizarre portrait. It was difficult to tell which part of the glowing octopus with the cat face was meant to be him. Bolognese Bumbler had been swept up in the abstract movement and was rewarded with a series of coloured blobs for his effort. Finally, Rapscallion Bumbler, the only self portrait to be found. Unless he happened to be a stick man in real life, then an artist he was not.

Perry disliked his name. It was bad enough being saddled with a surname like Bumbler, but the additional family custom of fanciful first names was extremely ill conceived, especially in modern times. He guessed he should be thankful he managed to avoid being called Asparagus-Starchild, or worse.

A far more worrying trend than exotic names, was the sad fact that Bumblers did not seem to enjoy much longevity. Even as

Perry neared reception, he passed more and more portraits of his unfortunate ancestors, all of whom had passed in peculiar circumstances. Death by raw vegetable, as in choking on a sprig of broccoli, courtesy of one Delectamundo Bumbler, a vegan of all things. Well, that taught her. And who could forget poor Convulsion Bumbler, who succumbed to a bolt of static electricity, whilst donning his all-in-one alpaca woollen romper suit. Perhaps the most perplexing of the lot was that of Juxtaposition Bumbler, who somehow managed to drown, whilst changing the water in a goldfish bowl.

Perry would be the first to admit he secretly bemoaned the fact his father's painting would never hang here, and even if he himself were to find fame and fortune, it would matter not. These walls were reserved for a different breed of individual. On a positive note, however, it might mean they both lived to a ripe old age, seldom a Bumbler hotel owner luxury it seemed.

And finally, here it was, hanging at the top of the stairs that led down into reception, his least favourite image in the entire collection, one Hugolicious Bumbler!

Uncle Hugo's cunning, but expansive face was laid bare for all to see. He was dressed in military uniform, adorned with outrageous epaulettes and a collection of medals so vast, it was superior work by the painter, not to present him totally lopsided. It was of course a complete and utter fantasy. The closest his uncle had ever come to the military was when he used to deliberately stand on, or kick, Perry's toy soldiers when passing.

To make matters worse, this was technically the second portrait his uncle had commissioned, the original now residing in the hotel's restroom, terrorising poor unsuspecting patrons. In an act of jaw dropping vandalism a moustache had been drawn on the painting. Quite understandably a previous guest had taken umbrage at Uncle Hugo's spikey personality and happened to have a marker pen to hand. It had all hideously backfired, as his uncle liked the look of it so much, he had attempted to grow his own and commissioned another rendering. That was a couple of years ago now, and he had to admit his uncle's moustache still looked as threadbare as when he first started cultivating it. It resembled a thin, slightly hairy slug, asleep on his upper lip. One that did not have the willpower, or inclination, to move again. A slug upon a slug thought Perry to himself, how fitting.

As he did most days, he resisted the urge to poke his finger through the painting and instead continued down the steps into the hotel reception.

I knew old Broadstroke, a great man. I once defeated him in an arm-wrestling contest, and for my troubles I won a bag of rare chicken teeth. I was also there on the day he won the most ridiculous challenge ever. I would tell you what it was, but you would not believe me. So just think of something ridiculous yourself, times it by ten and then stick a ridiculous jumper on it. I can assure you, it still will not be as ridiculous, but a good try, nevertheless. My favourite portrait is the exquisite likeness of Eucalyptus Bumbler. A little-known fact is that he posed for it on the toilet seat. He suffered from explosive diarrhoea for weeks, poor chap. Did I mention I am not a very good cook? I would also like to take this opportunity for an honourable mention of the following hotel owners young Perry omitted; Tadpole Bumbler – crushed in a chicken stampede, Crustacean Bumbler – assassinated in a high stakes Scrabble game, Pirouette Bumbler – allergic reaction to seaweed and finally, Abhorrent Bumbler – died of thirst whilst swimming the English Channel. HB

Chapter 5

Perry skipped down the final set of steps into reception. It was a large airy room that served the hotels entrance and led off to a dining room on the left and the drawing room on the right. The walls were all dark wooden panelling, from which hung a random series of coats of arms, crests, and shields, giving it all the look and feel of a stately manor.

The floor of black and white checks was freshly cleaned and polished, and it reminded Perry of happier days when he used to play games of giant chess upon it with his father. Huge navy-blue pots, overflowing with jungles of greenery and giant leaves, littered the room. In the right corner next to the entrance was a fake elephant foot, currently holding a series of weathered and battered looking umbrellas. On the left side of the door stood a short and stout suit of armour adorned with various dents and rust spots.

If Perry did not know better, he would have assumed his uncle had simply bought it off the internet, but according to his father, and confirmed on the information stand which stood before it, the previous owner was one Violet-Palava

Bumbler. She had been one of the few female hotel owners. Renowned and feared across the land for her shockingly bad temper and determination to fight anyone and everyone in mortal combat. She had been completely undefeated as it turned out, but apparently her horse had grown tired of lugging her around in that heavy suit of armour, and somehow managed to kick her down the side of a mountain.

The ticking of the grandfather clock, which stood inside the drawing room, could still be heard, such was the hushed silence that pervaded the morning. Perry saw that his dad was already hard at work, behind the impressive mahogany reception desk. It was another original feature of the hotel and although lovingly polished everyday, its many years of service could be counted in the numerous scratches and pockmarks that littered it.

If the hotel could be classed as a ship, then his father was unquestionably the captain of it. Although his father and uncle were twins, fate decreed that Uncle Hugo was the eldest by six minutes and the hotel was therefore his. The expectation was that his father would set out to forge his own destiny, but instead he had chosen to remain and work for his brother. It was just as well, as his father often had to reign in Uncle Hugo's rather rash eccentricities for the good of the hotel.

Perry could see the gleaming bald spot on his father's head which was currently buried in a thick ledger, no doubt looking at future bookings and tallying receipts. He had learned his trade when he was Perry's age and had been doing it ever since. It was all old school here at the hotel. No fancy computers or much else technology related. This was another thing his father would love to have changed, if only he was allowed. His many attempts to drag the hotel out of the past were always rebuffed.

But he just loved his job and the hotel so much. As such he tolerated his brother's antics, much to Perry's mother's annoyance. Like it or not this place was in his fathers DNA and when the truth finally got out, Perry was uncertain just how his dad would take the news.

'How are you doing son?' his father asked, having just noticed his presence. As always, he was immaculate in his pressed grey suit, his polished name badge shone.

'I'm fine dad,' Perry could not keep the sigh from his mouth, 'would be better if mum was here.' His father froze.

'I know, I know, she will be back soon, everything will be okay, I promise Perry.'

Perry just stared at his dad. The silence grew.

'So where are you off to so early, in that lovely ensemble, did you forget it's the weekend?' His dad looked down at his paperwork as he absent-mindedly rubbed the thin, decades old scar, on the side of his forehead.

'I'm just popping down to the village, I need to speak to Malaika about something.'

'Well, you have fun, but don't be too long, we will need you back here for lunch.'

'No worries dad, I'm really looking forward to it.' He hoped the smile that broke out on his face would fool his father.

It seemed to, as his dad smiled back warmly, small wrinkles forming at the corners of his eyes.

Perry was the first to admit that on looking at them both you would struggle to guess that his dad and Uncle Hugo were twins, never mind identical ones. His father's overly busy work schedule had him running around all day, which over the years had left him fit and trim, although he now wore reading glasses, and what was left of his hair was now salt and pepper in colour.

It had been called Dr Gupta's Concentration Crown and was all the rage a couple of years ago. It had all the benefits of a relaxing meditation, while making the mind sharper, even helping to raise ones IQ. His father, and so many others, wore it religiously, but he also invested family money into the venture. Whether it worked or not was soon to become irrelevant, because one of the immediate and unexpected side effects was permanent hair loss.

It was a complete disaster. Dr Gupta had to go into hiding in disgrace, investors lost their savings and thousands of people now had permanent bald spots and looked like trainee monks. It was yet another thing for his mother and father to row about, especially as it meant they were more dependent on Uncle Hugo than ever.

This only emboldened his uncle who just barked orders at them all day. All whilst his most strenuous activity was running a finger over random objects looking for dust - just so he could shout at people even more. As such he had put on an impressive amount of weight and insisted on wearing his hair slicked back like it was the 1930's. The addition of the ridiculous fledgling moustache only helped differentiate him further.

Perry certainly could not complain however, he would have found it too mentally exhausting having to dislike someone who was identical looking to his lovely father.

Uncle Hugo had many faults but undoubtedly his biggest, odious attitude aside, was his taste in clothing. Why would you want to wear something totally unsuitable. Absolutely ridiculous. Utterly bemusing. When you could change your attire as many as three or four times a day to pad out the whole farcical experience.

Before Perry had a chance to utter goodbye to his father he saw a flash of movement from the corner of his eye, something was standing at the head of the stairs.

'**FORE...,**' came the deafening cry.

I have stayed at this hotel various times back in the day. In fact, on one very wild afternoon, after too much sherry trifle, I did a spot of breakdancing in that very suit of armour. It was where the majority of the dents and scrapes came from, but no one will ever know. HB

Chapter 6

Both Perry and his father jumped as the cry echoed throughout reception. Perry looked to the top of the stairs and felt his heart drop, it was his Uncle Hugo.

The oafish lump stood there sporting a red plaid flat cap adorned with a pompom on top. A green diamond patterned sweater vest was stretched across his impressive girth. A truly horrendous pair of mustard plus fours ended just below his knees, where it was the responsibility of a pair of long purple socks to finish the shocking display. He was also tottering about in a pair of white golfing shoes. Overall, it was a deeply disturbing picture and an afront to all serious golfers everywhere. He looked like an enormous parrot, and this was only outfit number one of the day.

'Boy,' he spat, 'I'm surprised to see you up this early. What a state your hair is in. I want it washed and combed by lunchtime. There's no way that good hat I procured will have room to sit on your unruly head otherwise.'

'Good morning, Uncle Hugo, yes I'll make sure I do,' trilled Perry. He could not force his eyes away from the sight before him. His uncle certainly looked as if he was off to play a round of golf, although Perry had never seen his uncle swing a club in his life.

'Morning Hugo,' joined in his dad who briefly lifted his head above the ledger and did a double take at his brother's outfit.

'How are things looking this morning, are you on top of things?' commanded Hugo, as he took a pretend golf swing at a fictional golf ball.

This was how his uncle often spoke to Perry's father. It certainly was not how brothers should address each other; it was instead a boss talking down to an employee. Perry could feel his blood starting to boil at the sound of his uncle's pompous little voice.

'It's beginning to ramp up,' replied his father smiling and putting down the ledger, completely unphased by his brother's mannerisms. 'We actually had one guest arrive late last night, but Grubbins and Belinda had all the rooms ready in good order, everywhere has had a good clean and dusting.'

'Yes, I should think so too,' bleated Uncle Hugo. 'It's looking a little better around here, of course it should never be getting into that state anyway, guests or no guests.' He took another imaginary swing and almost toppled as he overbalanced.

'There is a sales conference in a couple of days, over in Tillybrook,' continued his dad.

'And how many more do we have due to arrive today or do I need to find out for myself?' queried Uncle Hugo. Another wild swing taken.

'Sorry, we should have three new guests arriving by lunchtime and a further four tomorrow. I did just hear on the radio however, there is a bad storm brewing, I'm hoping that doesn't cause us any issues.'

'Typical,' fumed Uncle Hugo, 'our first guests of the season and a possible storm to rain on our parade.' He now slashed his non-existent club back and forth in a frenzy, as if he were trapped in an invisible sand bunker.

'I'm sure it will be fine Hugo, the hotel is fully stocked, both Belinda and Grubbins know what needs to be done and we will have more staff on hand from tomorrow. We have done this many times, it will all run like clockwork.'

Perry certainly believed him. His dad was great at his job. He knew he would have thought of everything. Plus, all the staff loved him, quite possibly the only reason they continued to work here. His uncle would be in such a pickle if he ever left. Perry felt a lump in his stomach on touching that taboo subject again.

'Okay, well it better or I'll be holding you accountable,' Uncle Hugo huffed. He was now wiggling his bottom like an overactive duck as he lined up another phantom putt.

'I also heard there is going to be a big foodie gathering over in Gribditch in a couple of months. Your favourite chef will be attending.'

'What, not Barff Bartholomew?'

'The one and only.'

'I love his quintuple cooked chips,' drooled Uncle Hugo.

'It's just a shame about the quintuple chin they give you,' joked his father.

Uncle Hugo winced at the accusation, causing him to miss his illusion of a shot. 'Where about in Gribditch? Surely not in Bobby...'

'Random's hotel, yes,' finished Erstwhile.

'Well, that's no good, that Bobby Random is a crook, how is he raking in all that money going to help us?'

Perry could plainly see that the very idea of a business rival doing well, was causing a veritable rage to build inside his uncle, as his face slowly began to change shade.

'Because his prices are extortionate Hugo, and I plan to undercut him and make it widely known ahead of the event. The guests may well be attending his little convention, but they will be staying here before and after.'

'Excellent,' purred Uncle Hugo. His face had a slack lackadaisical look, which for him resembled deep concentration, and he made another fabricated shot. His hand punched the air when the imaginary ball fell into the non-existent cup. 'Perhaps we could send Belinda, she might pick up a few tips.'

'If only,' muttered Perry's father. 'Never mind the quintuple cooked chips, I would be happy if she could cook them properly the first-time round. Remember when...'

'No, we made a deal we wouldn't talk about that dinner again,' announced Uncle Hugo.

They say, after a nuclear war, the common cockroach would be the only survivor. This was a similar principle to Belinda's kitchen, where anything that survived her cooking, would find nuclear Armageddon a walk in the park.

In obvious high spirits after his mythological round of golf, Uncle Hugo carefully descended the stairs and tottered off in the direction of the dining room.

'I'm off to find Grubbins, he served me a rather fine port last night, I need to make sure he's not planning on serving that to any of the guests. We won't be making much of a profit if we give away all the good stuff,' and with that he waddled out of sight.

Perry and his father just stared at each other, there was no need for comment, such scenes were an everyday occurrence at the High Hill Hotel.

Perry turned to leave; he was on a tight schedule.

'Oh son, keep an eye on the weather, it's going to take a turn for the worse later.'

With that Perry gave his dad a backward wave as he opened the hotel door and stepped into the outside world. It was quite chilly and was already looking overcast. Perry pulled up his hoodie and bounced down the large steps, past the two silent stone lions that guarded the hotel, affectionately known as Benny and Bunny, and set off across the crunchy driveway on the long walk down to the village.

Perry however was unaware of the unblinking eyes that were watching him depart from the hotel, hidden deep in the thick of the nearby undergrowth. They stared...

What a nasty piece of work that Hugo Bumbler is. But I do like that outfit. I once had a hole in one whilst playing golf. The gusset of my trousers that is. I never realised there was so much bending over required. Luckily, my long overcoat hid the minor distraction. Oh, I said I liked the attire, I never said I would wear it. And another thing. Why stop at quintuple cooked chips when they can be cooked, oh let us say ten times! I will admit I did try this, and it was a total disaster, all I was left with was a pile of burnt carbon. Now, did you know that carbon, under pressure, results in diamonds. I had my cousin Asquith put those carbon remains in his trouser pockets. He always claims he is under enormous pressure at work. In 2,000 – 3,000 years I am going to have a nice little nest egg for my retirement. HB

Chapter 7

Currently devoid of any guest cars, Perry took quick crunching steps across the gravely courtyard and turned to look back, for he had a funny feeling he was being watched. Of course, there was nothing there, just the grand hotel with its gothic towers and pillars and the long shadows that fell before it. With its now darkly stained stone, Perry was the first to admit it could look a little creepy at times. That said, this time last year they had held a vampire inspired wedding reception, so it did have its plus points.

The High Hill Hotel was nestled on the outskirts of the sleepy village of Little Didwob, which itself sat amongst numerous neighbouring villages, towns, and city centres. Its beautiful location and scenery meant guests were more than willing to stay here and travel on to their ultimate destination. Soon there would begin an endless string of conventions, conferences, parades, galas, and sporting events that would bring people far and wide to their door.

The hotel was surrounded by a thick forest which in turn was surrounded by the Didwob river. Access to and from the hotel could only be gained by crossing the 'Ferryman's' bridge, Perry had no idea why it was called that, not that it was uppermost in his mind. Perry instead was thinking back to the history project both Malaika and himself had been working on.

He had rejected her initial idea and had instead gone with a dry and turgid report entitled 'Ebb and Flow - The Rising Tides of the Didwob River', which had gained them a semi respectable C+, although he was first to admit it was mostly down to Malaika and her genius idea to have it laminated. All teachers love a bit of lamination.

Their original discussion on the project was well over six months ago now and as he strode along the bridge, over the very river they wrote about, he racked his brain trying to remember everything, playing back the conversation they had. The conversation that gave Perry a sliver of hope that there might be a way out of this mess for his family.

Queue wobbly special effects as we drift back in time... HB.

They had both been in Malaika's bedroom, juice boxes in hand. Perry was sitting on the bed while Malaika stood and took centre stage. Her hair was held in two bunches, and she toyed with one of them absentmindedly, eager to begin and show off her hard work.

'Okay, so we know why we are here, are you ready?'

'Oh yes, I've had this moment highlighted on my calendar for a while - our soon to be award winning history assignment.'

Malaika was beaming which lit up her brown skin and made her hazel eyes twinkle. Perry could not help but smile back, she didn't do it very often in school due to the set of braces she had to endure, but they were due to come off in a couple of weeks and besides, they were best friends, who better to share a smile with. She took a step over to her wall where a mysterious tea towel was hanging.

'Ah yes, I was wondering what all that was about,' said Perry. 'This is a lovely bit of theatre I have to admit.' He put down his drink and started to give a polite clap until Malaika gave a cough for silence.

'Ladies and gentlemen,' she began, 'as per the minutes from our last meeting, it was agreed that as the brains of this outfit, I would source a topic so incredible, so monumental, so stunning in its scope and grandeur that a pass mark of over 50% would almost, perhaps, just may, be guaranteed on our history assignment.'

'Wow, you are really filling me with confidence,' said Perry.

'Enough of the heckling at the back,' replied Malaika. 'So, as I was saying before being rudely interrupted, I present to you option... number one.'

With that she whipped off the tea towel to reveal an unevenly cut rectangular piece of cardboard which was hanging by a bit of string pinned to the wall.

'Is... that it?' queried Perry, unsure of what he was looking at. 'Permission to properly heckle with a harangue thrown in as well.'

'Permission denied, look closely,' said Malaika.

Perry raised himself from the bed and stepped right up to the wall, his nose almost pressing up against the piece of cardboard.

'Yes, there it is, I see it now, I'm sorry for doubting you, it's some form of stamp.'

It was not a stamp however, instead it was a tiny black and white photocopy of a badly drawn, perhaps an etching, of what seemed to resemble a castle.

'It's not...'

'Yes, indeed it is, the great majestic Didwob Castle in all its past glory and splendour. Without it, in the eyes of our jealous neighbours, we became a lot less important and soon they referred to us as *Little* Didwob, may their ancestors rile in torment.'

'Mmmmm....,' was all Perry could muster.

'As you know I like to help out at the library and Mrs Salmon gave me some old books to look through and here you go, I found this marvellous picture.'

'Stunning....,' was all Perry could summon, and even then, he felt he was over egging it.

From the look on Malaika's face it was clear she felt she was quickly losing her audience.

'An important piece of our historical past. A strong fortification against the forces of evil. A castle sadly looted; its illustrious glory crushed to the ground. All that remains are tales of hidden treasure and of course, the ghost...'

Perry raised his hands to stop her. Thankfully, she did. He enjoyed the few moments of silence and took another loud slurp from his straw.

'Okay, very quickly there are three things that spring to mind. Number one, the hotel, my family's hotel, was built on top of those ruins. It's all gone and forgotten about, not interesting, even in the slightest.

Two, I have lived in that hotel all my life. There is no hidden treasure. If there were any then the Vikings or whoever looted the place, back in the time of the dinosaurs, took it all with them.

Three, there is NO ghost haunting the place. Okay, yes, my dad did tell me that Uncle Hugo did see something once, and there are certain parts of the building he won't set foot in, but it's never been seen since, or by any sane person for that matter. There is NO ghost.

Four...'

'Hang on,' said Malaika interrupting, 'I thought you said three things?'

'And four,' laboured Perry, 'this is a shockingly terrible idea. We only have a copy of a miniscule picture, that for the record looks like it was drawn by the left hand, of a right-handed child who was using a lump of coal instead of a pencil. We have hidden treasure that doesn't exist and a ghost that doesn't haunt. So, what else do we have? Is this the full extent of our potential history project?'

'I will admit,' replied Malaika slowly, clearly trying to choose the right words, 'that under cross examination there may be a few weak spots, a couple of gaps in the overall narrative but...'

'But what?' said Perry with an air of superiority.

'It was always my second choice,' she cried.

As quick as a whip she flipped the piece of cardboard over, punched Perry playfully in his arm (which surprisingly hurt, although he did his best not to show it) and jumped on the bed. All with an air of superiority, which made Perry's earlier air of superiority, look like the superiority a country bumpkin holds over a mildly clever turnip.

Perry stood there, his eyes agog, trying to take in the scene that lay before him. This was all to do with the robbery and the stolen museum exhibit, still to this day uncovered and believed to be hidden at his uncle's hotel.

BANG, BANG...

More wobbly special effects, if there is budget left... HB.

Before Perry could dwell on his reminiscing he was forced back to the present. He dived to the ground as gun shots rang out around him.

BANG, BANG...

———•◎•———

I do apologise for the interruption but what tops a potential assassination? I will tell you. Vikings riding Dinosaurs, that is what! A stunning idea. Right, you do whatever it is you need to do, while I go off and work on a new book plot. So excited. HB

Chapter 8

BANG, BANG...

The shots rang out in the still morning air, causing a flock of crows in the nearby field to take off in alarm.

BANG, BANG...

Came a repeat volley.

Perry went from stunned indecision to outright terror and hugged the ground even tighter. He could not believe that someone would want to shoot at him.

Taking pot shots from afar?

A mad sniper looking for another target?

Could it be Farmer Wilkie? Was he shooting at something?

It did not sound like a shotgun though. More like a blunderbuss, and to be quite honest Perry did not even know what that would sound like.

With nothing better to do he lay there pondering the wide and varied spectrum of possibility and probability. Including the fact, it could have been Farmer Wilkie's overfed cow Lizzy, suffering a bout of explosive flatulence. But that would have been stretching reality very thin indeed.

Speaking of which, Perry heard his shoes give off another fart like squeak, as if in sympathy. He then quickly apologised, to no one in particular, when he remembered he was no longer walking. It was in fact a naturally fear related response generated by himself.

BANG, BANG...

Another two shots! Worryingly, they both sounded louder. Was the shooter getting closer? Perry had been well on his way to the village now, he was on a lonely road with nothing but flat sparse field to either side, there was no hiding place. He was a sitting duck.

Over the horizon Perry noticed a plume of dirty grey swirling smoke appear. Gun smoke thought Perry to himself, gulping hard. Just then a motorcycle shot into view, rising over the small hill, approaching him. It shuddered and shook, struggling with its heavy load and from the look of it, old age. This was a vintage motorcycle and it had a sidecar affixed, which looked full of luggage and boxes. The shivering, shuddering device slowed down and stopped next to him, as if out of breath.

BANG, BANG...

Perry coughed and covered his mouth as the cloud of exhaust fumes engulfed him.

'I'm... I'm looking for directions,' came the shrill cry of the mysterious rider, 'that is if you have finished your press-ups or whatever it is you are up to.'

Perry realised he looked ridiculous, still lying on the ground. He coughed again and slowly rose to his feet, his eyes were now beginning to water with the smog the vibrating bike was belching out.

The stranger was wearing, of all things, a brown leather flying cap and aviator goggles, over a pair of thick brown spectacles, along with a pair of long brown gloves. He also sported a lengthy brown leather trench coat. He looked as if he had just landed a biplane from World War I.

He proceeded to lift the goggles on to the top of his head which offered Perry the opportunity to study him further. He modelled a bowl cut of thin stringy, greasy looking brown hair which dangled over his sweaty forehead like vines. He had an ordinary placid face, with pock marked cheeks and like his uncle, sported a moustache from the school of unflattering facial hair. It looked as if he had taped a brush head above his lip, the hairs as thick as bristles. It all ended unspectacularly in a weak wobbly little chin.

Through the gaps in his outer wear, Perry noticed he was resplendent in a brown suit, brown tie, and brown brogues. Even his eyes were brown! It had only been a matter of seconds, but Perry could already sense an interesting combination of timid mousy insecurity with deranged overtones.

'Are... are you... Mr... Brown?' Perry asked tentatively, and why not, if ever a name was deserved. He waited for the man's mouth to open. When it did Perry had to quash his excitement. Brown-stained teeth. With quite a gap between the front two.

'Sorry... Sorry,' replied the individual.

'Apologies, just a wild guess on my part,' said Perry.

'No... No, I'm Sorry... Sorry Noakes. I'm looking for directions. I'm looking for the High Hill Hotel.' He stared at

Perry. 'DO - YOU - UNDERSTAND - ME?' He began speaking slowly and loudly, looking at Perry as if he had just found the village simpleton. Perry meanwhile was lost in thought, the gap in his teeth gave Mr Noakes voice a slight musical whistling tone.

Perry wiped his now dirty hands, on his now dirty trousers and thought he would have a little fun.

'I understands. I do. I surely do. Indeedy,' replied Perry in a quickly made-up voice.

'Yes... Yes, well, I'm looking for the High Hill Hotel, I believe it's around these parts somewhere. Although I do have to say, that on current elevation, and I have been charting it don't you know, that this hotel is unlikely to be on a hill nor very high. I'm willing to bet I'm going to be disappointed.'

'Oh, that where ye be wrong. Indeedy. Indeedy do,' uttered Perry, trying to keep a straight face. 'Don't let this path fool ye, ye are in the right direction fer sure. Indeedy do. Why, in just a few turns an twists, an more turns and a little twist and another turn around a twist, why ye will find yerself higher than a kite. Indeedy.' Perry turned in the direction of travel and went to point.

'Why, indeedy, just behind that line of trees ye will see...,' but Perry stopped. There were no trees to be seen. Just large grey clouds that had descended. They had crept up behind him on his way down to the village, like a thick veil of fog, or a hundred of Mr Noakes belching motorcycles. The view was completely blotted out by smoky tendrils.

'Indeedy. Just take my words for it. Indeedy do. Continue on this path and you can't miss it, just over the bridge and you will be there, but be careful...'

'Careful... Careful?' replied Sorry Noakes rather nervously, 'careful about what exactly?'

'Oh, it be steep. Indeedy. Did ye know they keep an oxygen bottle by the sides of the bed in case you get all lightheaded? Indeedy. People have even sworn they have seen angels floating about outside their windows, on account they be so high up. The place does get great reviews so I hears. Indeedy do. To be true they may have been hallucinating while they wrote them, I've never dared to stay there me self. Indeedy. Well, not a second time that is. I never felt quite right after the last time when I was rushed to hospital. Altitude sickness it was. Indeedy. Serves me right for not using the air tank. Indeedy. Indeedy do.' For extra effect Perry then threw in a donkey like laugh. Sorry Noakes was visibly shaken.

'Well... Well, emmm, yes, thank you. I had better get off, good day to you.'

It took him a few attempts to nervously kick start his bike, but soon he was off, disappearing in a plume of acrid smoke, before fading out of sight amongst the low hanging mist.

BANG, BANG...

———●◎●———

He was a strange fellow; I wonder if we will be seeing him again? As we are on the subject, I do find the colour brown to be rather dull, do you? Perhaps in his spare time he likes to stand up against garden fences and blend in like a chameleon. I am now trying to remember how much wood panelling the hotel has. They may not even realise he is standing there trying to check in. HB

Chapter 9

Perry rubbed at the dirty knees of his trousers and marched on.

SQUEAK... **SQUEAL...** **CHEEP...**

SQUEAK... **SQUEAL...** **CHEEP...**

Soon he was entering the charming and quintessential village of Little Didwob. Full of picturesque chocolate box cottages, cobbled streets, a market square, cricket pitch and more hedges than you could shake a stick at. To be honest, it was just as floral, quaint, and fair as all the other villages that surrounded it. One thing they did not possess, however, much to their jealousy, was a very grand and prestigious hotel within their borders. That said, another thing they did not possess, much to their delight, was a prolonged, persistent, and progressive poo problem!

For months now piles of it were suddenly appearing, dotted across the length and breadth of the village. Many at first thought a horse had escaped, such was the sheer size and volume being deposited, but it did not take a forensic examination to quickly rule that out. It had to be a dog. An exceptionally large dog. But who's dog? Who would take their dog out for a walk in a lovely place like Little Didwob and not pick up afterwards, it simply was not done. It was not the Little Didwob spirit.

With the culprit still at large, things began to escalate. Suspicion reigned. Neighbour spied on neighbour. Paranoia was prevalent. Whole families fell out with each other. But still the issue persisted. Let your guard down for one moment and SQUELCH, you suddenly had a nasty problem on your hands, or the sole of your shoe at the very least. The children in the village, quite rightly, found this sort of thing absolutely hilarious, especially if they were lucky enough to come across the unfortunate footprints of an unlucky victim.

Once the villagers of Little Didwob had grown tired of blaming their own, they started looking further afield and began accusing the surrounding communities. It was because they were bitter and envious of their lovely village they claimed. Some even believed visitors were bringing it in with them in the dead of night and lobbing it about the streets like deranged monkeys.

Others, mostly the weird ones, were certain it was some mythical wild animal that was preying on the village. Having to watch where you stepped during the day was small fry in comparison to running into the great devilish beast in person.

Then the mystery was solved. By sheer chance. An actual sighting of the culprit. It wasn't some spiteful neighbouring visitor, nor was it a horrid monster from the depths of a nightmare, a huge saliva dripping wolf down from the forest or an intergalactic pooping alien from outer space. Instead, it was a small stray dog that had wandered into their village one day, and for the moment, didn't seem to be in a hurry to leave. Well, not until it had left its mark. And boy did it leave many of them.

Despite its tiny size, it was mischievous enough to leave its stunningly large bottom gifts just around blind corners, or even on an unsuspecting doorstep. No one in the village was clever enough to counter its devious cunning. The residents were warned not to feed him, and it would soon be on its way, or at the very least run out of ammunition. But Perry had caught Malaika red handed throwing it handfuls of biscuits and he also knew she had left it plates of treats hidden under various hedges across the village. No wonder it was still hanging about. She was a soft touch that one.

As Perry continued through the streets and alleyways towards Malaika's home, he ensured all was clear before him. Sweeping his eyes right and left for any natural land mines. For the record, Pretzel, as Malaika had now named him, had the distinction of being the only village resident to be officially banned from the hotel. Obviously bored with causing daily carnage in the village, Pretzel had somehow made his way up last week and by the time he was spotted he had left a series of chocolate kisses across the carpets, much to the annoyance of Uncle Hugo. Grubbins was less than charmed as well considering he was the one ordered to clean it all up. Perry guessed that if Uncle Hugo owned a safari suit, and it was surely only a matter of time, he would have set off down to the village to go hunting after it.

As it turned out, Perry's carefully trodden path through the village was quite uneventful and he made it to Malaika's door unscathed. He knocked on it loudly. Malaika's mother was a cleaner and would already be out to work. With it being a Saturday however it would not have surprised Perry if Malaika was still asleep in bed. He felt guilty but it had to be done.

'Perry,' cried Malaika as she opened the door, 'what a lovely surprise, did we have something on today?'

'No, apologies, this is all on me, I'm sorry about the early start but I just had to see you.' He found his voice was getting tight and he hoped he was not going to start crying. Malaika quickly ushered him in.

'I'll take my shoes off. I think I managed to avoid anything nasty, but better safe than sorry,' he said.

'Yes, young Pretzel had better watch himself, he's been outdoing himself lately, my Mum said the village committee are thinking of getting someone in to deal with him.'

Two cans of fizzy pop liberated from the fridge later and they were up in Malaika's bedroom, music from the radio turned down to a manageable background buzz. Malaika had her hair in her normal bunches and wore a pair of blue dungarees, a striped t-shirt, and high tops.

'So, what's bothering you, Perry? Isn't the hotel properly open now? You aren't skiving, are you? Had enough already, off to join the circus and coming to say goodbye?'

'It's my uncle,' wheezed Perry through gritted teeth.

'What about him? Aside from being a rude greedy bully, with a shocking dress sense...,' she stopped, sensing that Perry wasn't playing along.

'He's trying to sell the hotel,' Perry blurted out. He felt like he had been holding it in forever and it was great to finally release the growing pressure. 'Sell it. The family hotel. After all these years.'

'Okay,' said Malaika calmly, 'why don't you start from the beginning.'

'In the evenings Grubbins prepares a drink for Uncle Hugo and some of those little bits of cheese on a stick. Well, a few nights ago I offered to take it up to him. When I went into his office, he wasn't there so I put it all on the desk for him. I know I shouldn't have but I couldn't help it. There was lots of paperwork on there, all spread out, so I had a little look. A couple of invoices, some fashion stuff, holiday information, nothing too amazing. But then I found it, a legal letter about the proposed sale of the hotel and land to some company called Quantum Affiliation. There wasn't the time to read it fully, even if I had I'm not sure I would have understood it anyway, but I saw enough to know that he is in talks to sell it. Sell it all and move on.'

'Wow, I didn't know he could do that,' muttered Malaika.

'Neither did I, but he doesn't have any children, so no one to pass the hotel directly on to. If anything happened to him it should go directly to my father, but it seems he would much rather sell it. He only cares about himself.'

'What are you going to do?'

'After the initial surprise I was happy, unbelievably. Without the hotel, no more Uncle Hugo, my mum and dad would get back together again. We could have a normal life together, just like everyone else.'

'And then...'

'And then I got angry, I surprised myself. How dare he sell the hotel that has been in our family forever. The news would devastate my dad, and before you ask, I have not told him; not yet. That's when I got the idea... Malaika, I need your help. I need you to help me save the hotel.'

I feel for Pretzel's victims, I really do. Nothing like walking about town, taking pride in your footwear, especially if they have an expensive and superior tread. Standing in a small poo mountain surely deflates one's moral. You may as well throw them away. Wash them and try and pick out the brown bits with a used lolly stick all you want, but you will never get it all out. The stigma of the 'poo shoe' will forever remain. You will be haunted by a phantom smell and will be paranoid ever after. HB

Chapter 10

Hugo did his best to stride through the drawing room with vigour and purpose, but he had severely underestimated the limitations of golf shoes on carpet. Also, the sudden gloom that had permeated and overtaken the room was not helping either. A quick look over at the patio doors revealed an increasing number of dark clouds forming outside and quite possibly fog. His know-it-all brother was correct again, as usual. He took a mental note to have Erstwhile or his useless son Perry clean all the toilets later. That cheered Hugo up no end, he cracked a thin cruel smile.

'Ah, there you are Grubbins,' he said to the man behind the small bar who had been polishing a glass within an inch of its life.

Grubbins was the hotel bartender, the hotel caretaker, the hotel odd job person extraordinaire. He was a small lean man with watery blue eyes. His hair was thin, grey, and receding but there was still enough of it to wear back in a small ponytail. Grubbins ruddy complexion was partially hidden behind two enormous billowing side chops.

'Now pay attention Grubbins, you simple spec of insignificance,' sneered Hugo.

'Here M'lud.'

'Yes, yes, I smelled you several hours ago. Speaking of which I have a telegram here from the palace. The King commands you to have a bath. Immediately. He swore he could smell you this morning and was quite unable to finish his breakfast of porridge and prunes. Grubbins, you are causing our monarch to lose weight.'

'I'm terribly sorry M'lud. I'll douse myself down with the wet rag again.'

'Please do, and when you have finished make sure that rag is burned, and its remains buried in secret. I will not have it fall into the hands of terrorists as some form of biological weapon.'

'Yes M'lud.'

'Now, go off and see how Belinda is doing in the kitchen, she may need some help.'

'At once M'lud,' said Grubbins who shuffled out of the room.

Hugo closed his eyes, appreciating the quietness of the morning, the silence of the...

'Why, hello there,' came a fragile voice from nowhere.

Hugo's cap almost flew off his head, such was the force of his nervous jerk. He could have sworn he was alone in the room, but the lack of light had camouflaged an intruder or something far worse. He looked timidly around.

'Over here,' came the voice again.

Hugo finally traced its origin. Yes, someone was sitting in one of the high-backed leather chairs. Sitting or was it sinking into it? The individual looked as old as parchment and as grey as the gathering clouds outside.

'Hello there, good morning,' Hugo beamed, flashing his well practiced, most fakest smile, which made his sparse moustache work hard to stretch across his bloated face. 'I hope you are enjoying your stay here at the High Hill Hotel?'

'I certainly am,' came the reply followed by a rictus grin which instantly set Hugo on edge. 'Would you like a crouton?' the old man held up a paper bag filled with what looked like crumbs. 'I love croutons. Like little dice made of toast. Brilliant. Mind you, they play havoc with these false teeth of mine though,' and with that he spat them into the wrinkled palm of his hand and began picking and scraping debris from between the gaps.

Hugo covered his mouth with his hand, he could feel his face turning green at the sickening sight being conducted before him. Simply revolting. Thankfully, the slimy grime encased false gnashers were finally popped back into the guests shrivelled mouth.

'I'm here for the sales convention over at Tillybrook,' continued the old man, not missing a beat, as if turning your mouth inside out was an everyday occurrence enjoyed by all and sundry. I've decided this will be my last one.'

Hugo found himself nodding, he could well believe it, the wizened man looked like he could collapse into a pile of dust at any minute.

'I was delighted when I realised, I would be able to reside here for a night or two.'

'Really,' perked up Hugo, 'I suppose we have come very highly recommended.'

'Not quite,' the salesman grinned back, a soggy bread infused grin at that. He then began grappling with the chair as he fought to free himself from its enveloping folds. Finally, he managed to prop himself up.

Hugo had the long and proud record of disliking each, and every single guest, who had ever set foot and resided within his hotel. It had only taken but a matter of minutes and this old husk of a man was starting to head to the top of the list.

The salesman shot out his hand with vigour towards Hugo. This caused an involuntary flinch which Hugo cursed himself for. To overcompensate, Hugo gripped the hand tightly and so began the age-old handshake wrestle. Hugo had to admit, the old fellow had quite a hold. Sweat was now beginning to break out on his forehead as he tried to increase the pressure, but it had no effect. Instead, with every passing second, it was his hand that was at risk. The old man's steel like grasp was getting increasingly painful. Finally, he had to accept defeat and managed to wrestle his hand free.

'I'm Gentle-Me. Seymour Gentle-Me, and in response to your statement...'

Mr Gentle-Me's eyes seemed to glaze over. Hugo stood waiting for him to finish his sentence, but nothing was forthcoming. It was as if someone had pressed a pause button. Hugo looked left and right as if this was some form of prank, but if it was there was no one else there to witness it. He took a small step backwards when...

'... no, not recommended, but I was once a guest here before. Many, many years ago. In fact, I was here, at this hotel on the very day you and your brother were born.' He flashed that grin again. At least this time it seemed devoid of crouton fragments.

'Obviously, I was much younger back then and I had the absolute pleasure of meeting your mother. A remarkable woman. She was expecting in a few weeks time, but you couldn't wait and had other ideas. It was all extremely exciting.'

'**HOT WATER!**' Seymour screamed, causing Hugo to recoil in shock.

'Excuse me?' said Hugo. He had no idea where this conversation was going, but he wanted it to end. He was beginning to question the sanity of Mr Gentle-Me.

'Hot water and towels. That's what they always shout for when someone goes into labour. That was my job. Now, if memory serves, I was just finishing a lovely plate of scrambled eggs with chives. Mmmmm...'

Seymour Gentle-Me's eyes seemed to glaze over again, and he fell silent. Hugo assumed his batteries were running low. He was debating whether to prod him, or better yet make an escape, when Mr Gentle-Me sprang back into life.

'Hot water was no problem. Neither were the towels, certainly not in a hotel. However, at the time I just happened to be selling the 'Nimbus'. It was the number one towel on the market with its patented fluffy cloud softnology. Quite luxurious and I had plenty to share.'

'Ah yes,' he grinned again, more rapturous than rictus this time. 'You and your brother, oh how the years have passed. Indeed, coming back here was too good an opportunity to pass up. I was however deeply sorry to hear about your mothers passing, a fine woman. We became friends of a sort after that day.'

'You... you did?' stammered Hugo.

Mr Gentle-Me slowly reached into the inside of his suit jacket and after an age, as if in a tug of war competition with his inside pocket, finally pulled out a bundle of yellowed envelopes, held together with a purple ribbon. There was a sudden smell of dusty crypt and the passage of time.

'We became pen pals; I believe that was the term for it back in the day. My business really took off that year. I've travelled the world several times over. Sold countless things. Made and lost fortunes. But the one thing I cherished above all was having your mother as a friend and confidant. She will be missed.'

'Yes, she is,' replied Hugo in the high art of lying, he missed the horrid woman not one bit.

'Well, if you excuse me Mr Gentle-Me, it was nice to meet you, but I am afraid there is no rest for the wicked.'

'Of course. Perhaps you could indulge me later. I would very much like to talk with you and your brother. It would be wonderful to converse with you both, I would love to share with you some of the charming updates your mother used to send me.' He patted the pile of envelopes that now rested on his lap.

'Err... yes,' said Hugo, who began to edge his way out of the room. Hugo had a bad feeling about this man. It looked like he was going to meddle in things best left alone...

Mr Seymour Gentle-Me, has been around the block a few times. He has sold everything from the Abacus to Zebra's. He was once rumoured to have been the manager of the Beatles before they became mildly famous. Do not bother looking them up, from memory they were a three-piece collective from Yorkshire, with their own brand of Reggae Folk music. I never realised he was a fan of the crunchy crouton. A much-maligned food group, never quite having the gravitas or standing it is due in the dried bread community. HB

Chapter 11

'You need me to save the hotel! I like the sound of that,' prompted Malaika.

'Well, you need to hear my idea first, I'll admit now it's weak and desperate, but it's all I have. The problem here is Uncle Hugo, he's the one that must go. But what if it was my dad who bought the hotel? Surely Uncle Hugo would sell it to him if he was getting the money he wanted. Then my dad would be the boss, the hotel could finally be run properly and with my uncle gone my mum would come back, we would run it together, the three of us.' Perry was going misty eyed at this fantasy version of the future.

'I'm sorry to burst your bubble Perry, but how much does your uncle pay your dad?'

'Not enough. Obviously, there is no way he could afford it. But that's where you come in.'

'Me! Sorry to disappoint Perry, but I'm afraid my savings are still decimated from all the parts I needed to buy for that metal detector.'

During the previous summer holidays, Malaika had spent her days scouring the sprawling grounds of the hotel with a metal detector that her mother had cobbled together. All she had found for her troubles and hard work were two spoons and a fork. As delighted as Uncle Hugo had been to bring them back into the fold, Malaika was bitterly disappointed with the whole experience. Perry was suddenly concerned that she might have put the whole thing to bed for good after that. He had only just noticed that the piece of cardboard was still on the wall, but not as he had last seen it.

It was now covered with pictures of that stupid boyband he could not stand, what did they call themselves again? It was something silly, even sillier than how they looked with their cheesy grins and coiffed hair. I bet their hair didn't stick up on end all day in protest like his did. They had things so easy. That was it, they called themselves Balooga Razzamatazz. Really! Malaika had now seriously fallen in his estimation.

Perry was now beginning to lose his nerve and looked to change the conversation. He turned his attention to a strange book that was lying on the bed next to him.

'Hey, what's this you are reading, and why is it wrapped in tinfoil or is this what was left of your braces after you got them off?'

'It's my journal charting strange occurrences and conspiracy theories,' replied Malaika, in complete deadpan seriousness.

'Of course, how could I forget, but I thought it was tinfoil hats that you people wore?'

'You can't be too careful,' replied Malaika. She made a point of going over to the bedroom window and looking outside for any parked vehicles which may have been secretly listening to them. 'Needless to say, I could still balance it on my head if some passing spy satellite was trying to read my mind.'

'And does that happen often then?' Before Malaika could reply to Perry he had opened the book at a random page and fired off another question. 'What's all this about? The Didwob Leech!'

'Ah yes, but it's more of a serpent to be honest. It was supposed to terrorise the Didwob river, the very one that encircles your hotel. They say it was another smart reason to build the castle there. I mean, after fighting off a sea monster who would have the strength to then walk up that hilly hill.'

'Okay, okay,' said Perry. He proceeded to skim read page after page. 'What about this one? The Floating Skull of Nimble Lane!'

'Oh, that's a good one,' replied Malaika. 'Several witnesses all came forward, all upstanding members of the community with no reason to lie. It floated there in the dark, green ectoplasm streaming out of its eye sockets and it chased people up and down the lane.'

'Okayyy...,' said Perry clearly not believing a word of it. 'The Werewolf of FlatRock Bay. FlatRock Bay as in the one a few miles from here?'

'Indeed,' smiled Malaika, 'and I have heard its howl once myself, the wind carried the haunting cry on the night air.'

'More likely you heard Grubbins after trying one of his experimental cocktails,' and as if to prove his point, Perry took a big swig of fizzy pop and gave a thunderous belch. Malaika bent over laughing.

Perry reconsidered. He felt the old Malaika was still there, and she had not changed. In a bold move he stood up from the bed and walked over to the hanging cardboard, with its annoying band members, and turned it over.

Perry stood there, his eyes agog, trying to take in the scene that lay before him. This side of the board looked like something from a TV show or a film. It was full of pictures of people and places familiar to Perry. The hotel and the museum. There were yellowed newspaper clippings. And string. Lots and lots of string. Assorted colours held in by pins. Some linking one item to another, showing some form of a relationship to others. It was wild and intricate. It was epic.

This is what he had come for. He should never have doubted her. Malaika was fascinated with this story. This and a lot of other theories, but to her this was the holy grail. This board told the story of the legendary museum robbery and the exhibit that was stolen. To this day still out there somewhere, waiting to be found. And the exciting part to this story was that many, particularly Malaika, thought it was hidden at his uncle's hotel.

'You really believe in all this don't you?'

'Yes, I really do,' said Malaika, quickly jumping off the bed, 'and I LOVE your idea.'

'You do?'

'Let me see if I've guessed it. If, I mean, WHEN we find the hidden treasure, at your odious uncle's hotel, we will collect a very substantial reward.'

'I... guess.'

'That reward money will then be used to procure said hotel, keeping it within the warm embrace of the Bumbler family. With the unlikeable and incompetent uncle out of the picture, its true potential can then be realised.'

Perry, as if he was four years old, began jumping up and down on the spot and started clapping.

'Mummy and Daddy Bumbler, back together again, reignite their love for each other and before you know it Perry finds himself spending his evenings babysitting his new little sister, Wilhelmina Rusty-Tap Bumbler.'

'What, eh?'

'Now disillusioned with life in the hotel and spurned by the love of his life Malaika Omari, Perry flees, only to endure a string of menial jobs, until he finally ends up working in a shoe shop, where he becomes addicted to the smell of sweaty feet.

'No, No... you're ruining it.'

Perry turned away and sat back down his face flushing red. 'I told you it was a weak idea, but I can't think of anything else. I'm desperate.

'Well, joking aside I don't think it's a stupid idea, I absolutely believe it is hidden up there somewhere and we need to find it,' said Malaika, as determined as Perry had ever heard her.

His face lit up. 'Okay then. Partners. If we find it, we split the reward 50/50.'

Malaika looked him up and down and gave him a puzzled look. 'I thought we were already partners?'

'Let's be honest Malaika, you are the one who was obsessed about all this. It was you that was going out all day on fruitless searches. To be honest, I've just been humouring you. I never truly believed in any of it.'

In truth he was quite tired of the story. The number of residents at the hotel who would grill them on the theory was absurd, obviously it had been far worse in his father's time.

'That may be true Perry, but if it wasn't for you, I would never be allowed anywhere near the hotel, inside or out. So, partners.'

Malaika and Perry each shook each others' pinkies in agreement.

'Well, it's time we took this seriously then, we need to step things up,' said an eager Perry.

'You don't mean what I think you mean,' gasped Malaika, who quickly sat down on the bed again, excitement buzzing through her.

'I think I do,' he replied. 'It could be dangerous and if my dad caught us, he would be furious, but it's time we visited the catacombs. We can't afford not to, there is too much riding on this.'

'That's great news,' shrieked Malaika hysterically. The old catacombs were the only part of Didwob Castle that remained after the hotel was built on top of it. She reached over and gave Perry a crushing hug.

'It's okay,' said Perry, who was going red in the face again from the sheer force of the embrace. 'I know where I can get the key. We can start looking early tomorrow morning, things will still be a little slow at the hotel, and I'll be able to slip away and help. If I was going to hide anything in that place, then it would be down there.'

'Agreed,' said Malaika.

'Okay,' said Perry starting to feel the excitement build. I know it was decades ago and the trail is stone cold but run it all past me again. Don't leave anything out.'

Malaika did not need to be asked twice and a massive grin broke out on her face.

'Almost 30 years ago there was a nefarious robbery. Only a couple of towns over from here, there was a break in at the Chumford museum. The Krustovia crown jewels were on display, it was part of an exhibit that was touring the country. It was a disaster. The diplomatic fall out. There was even talk of war at one point. Things have still never properly recovered. What was worse was the failure to recover them, despite capturing the culprit - one Sinclair Marx. Internationally renowned thief and cat burglar, better known as the infamous... Plimsoll Bandit.

I have nothing against people wanting to wear a tinfoil hat, but I will always stand by my fashionable fedora. I also have nothing against people wishing to be a critical thinker. The sad situation nowadays is that most conspiracy theories go by another name – spoiler alerts. HB

Chapter 12

'Also responsible for a string of high-profile robberies across the world and number one on every police force's most wanted list,' said Perry. He took another big swig of fizzy pop.

'Yes, yes,' said Malaika, 'but this was the big one, the one that led to his downfall and eventual capture. As usual he was scrupulous in his planning and was all prepared for another masterclass in heist pulling.'

'But?'

'But he had a little piece of bad luck,' continued Malaika.

'The Plimsoll Bandit crept along the floor. He rolled left. Cartwheeled right. Flopped backwards. Sprang forward. It was all choreographed.'

Malaika had now jumped onto the bed. Tiger like she was crouched in position ready to leap herself. Perry carried himself over to the corner of the room out of the way and watched her.

'He had mapped this out meticulously. He knew exactly where he needed to be and when. He had timed everything to perfection. He was aware of where every camera was situated. He understood every view they would take. More importantly, he knew all the blind spots. He had already disarmed the alarms, but he couldn't turn the cameras off or security in the control room would have been instantly aware. But it was fine. This is what he lived for; this is what he was born for. He was the best thief in the world.'

Malaika rolled along her bed.

'He spun and vaulted, rotated, and darted, lunged, and pirouetted. It was a remarkable sight. Staying in the shadows and evading the glare of the cameras as he got closer and closer to his prize. He was like a ghost.'

'You are describing this very well,' Perry had to admit, slightly concerned she was going to vault out of the window next.

'That's because I have seen it.'

'You have!'

'Yes, it's old news now. They have a copy of the footage down at the police station. The Sergeant let my mum borrow it to show me. She told him that I was going to find the treasure one day.'

Malaika's mother cleaned at a variety of places, the police station being one of them.

'Sorry, I didn't mean to interrupt you.'

'And then he stopped... He froze. He was undone! The smile slid from his confident face. He looked up and stared at it. One of the cameras wasn't moving. It was terrible luck to be fair. It was earlier that very morning; some kid at the museum with a ball. I mean what kind of parent allows their kid to take a ball to a museum? Well anyway, he had bounced it and in return it had hit the camera. Broken it. It was still filming but it was no longer rotating. There was no time to get it fixed. They felt they could live with it for one night. No real harm done. But for the Plimsoll Bandit it was the beginning of the end.

'It had been mostly filming him the entire time he was in the room. The film was in black and white, but I swear you could almost see the colour drain from his face. He wasn't even wearing a mask such was his confidence, or arrogance. He knew instantly the guards would be on their way, along with the police. There was no time left for subtlety. He just smashed the glass case and began to thrust the crown jewels into his backpack.'

Malaika stood on the bed scooping up invisible jewels and throwing them into an imaginary bag.

'His bald head was now beaded in sweat and his thin face was pinched. He was out of the room for about 10 seconds before the guards rushed in. From that point onwards he was a wanted man.'

'And they finally caught up with him, on the grounds of the High Hill Hotel.'

'Exactly, but missing the stolen items, which is why everyone believed he had hidden them there. He had been working at the hotel for a couple of weeks, posing as a labourer during its refurbishment. Very handy for being able to visit the museum every day, watching, learning, and plotting. It would have been so easy to have hidden them at the hotel, with all the work going on, no one would have been suspicious. Perhaps it was always a plan B for him in case something went wrong.'

'But the police never found it. They scoured the place, inside and out and recovered nothing.'

'Yes, the Plimsoll Bandit had many faults, which goes without saying, but he was clever, very clever.' Malaika jumped off the bed now that her demonstration was over. 'He's still in prison. His capture helped resolve a vast number of crimes committed far and wide. But it was his refusal to say where he had concealed the jewels that still has him locked up. Which is why...'

'The reward for finding the stolen exhibit is so high,' finished off Perry, his eyes lighting up. 'Enough to secure the safety of the hotel.'

As if sensing some foreboding the room was plunged into gloom.

'What happened?' asked Perry. 'Have all the planets aligned to form a doomsday eclipse? Is this in your book?'

'Oh my,' said Malaika, who pressed her face against the window. 'Just look at those clouds, like floating lumps of coal in the sky, the weather is about to definitely take a turn for the worse.'

'My dad did warn me there was a storm brewing.'

'Well, you better get off then, as great as it's been to see you today you don't want to get caught in that rain once it starts.'

As if to back up her claim a fat blob of water hit the pane at force, followed by another.

'You are right,' said Perry springing to his feet. 'Listen, this hoodie is pretty thin, is there any chance I could borrow...'

Malaika rolled her eyes.

A few minutes later Perry darted from the house as he made his way back up to the hotel. He was wearing a nifty tinfoil hat to keep off the rain, courtesy of one book cover and Malaika's origami prowess.

————•◎•————

Now gentle reader, this in the trade is called scene setting and I do hope you have been paying attention, as I shall be asking questions later. HB

Chapter 13

Perry had made his way back to the hotel in double smart time, but the heavens had well and truly opened and snazzy tinfoil hat aside, he was soaked through on his arrival. He darted upstairs, took a quick shower, fought a fierce battle with his hair - which he lost - and then, the ultimate humiliation, he put on his new uniform. But before he headed back downstairs, he had to make a small detour, there were a handful of items he had to source which would be vital for later in the day...

Now he found himself standing in the drawing room, a bemused look fixed firmly to his face. He was glad that the worsening weather outside had the room in partial darkness as he did his best impression of the Plimsoll Bandit, by trying to hide in the shadows. He mostly felt aggrieved at having to wear the silly hat which currently sat askew upon his head. Perry had been tempted to keep the tinfoil one, but best not to push his luck with Uncle Hugo on their opening day. There was always tomorrow.

Perry was straining to hold a large heavy silver tray laden with glasses of wine. His job was to effortlessly glide around the room, allowing everyone to help themselves to a beverage. To be more precise his focus was on not dropping the tray, a fate that had occurred on more than one occasion previously. Perry vowed it would not be happening today, he would not give his uncle the satisfaction of berating him, he would make his dad proud.

Unfortunately, to make matters worse, his new jacket was rather tight in all the wrong places, and it made elevating the tray even more difficult, but he struggled on. Besides, if he were to drop the tray, he would be doing everyone a massive favour. The wine on offer, it was fair to say, was not to be trusted.

Uncle Hugo jokingly referred to it as the 'wine cellar' but it was nothing more than a run-down wooden shack hidden at the back of the hotel, deep into the forest. This was where Uncle Hugo conducted his skulduggery. A large rusty vat consumed most of the available room and one of Grubbins tasks had been to keep it constantly filled with the cheapest, nastiest plonk, that Uncle Hugo could lay his hands on. This vicious cocktail of drink, which had a kick like cough medicine, was then repoured into more reputable looking wine bottles for use within the hotel, The ramshackle hut even had a little corking machine, which was the final addition to the duplicity. Perry and Malaika had both once sneaked in there for a look and had great fun playing around with it. He had even managed to get a cork right in her belly button to both their amusement.

'**Crumbs**....' spluttered Perry when his uncle waddled into the room alongside the guests.

As expected, he was now changed from the morning golfing attire, and had morphed himself into some wild thing from the upper reaches of the North. He was wearing a black jacket and waistcoat and was swathed in yards of yellow and black tartan that made up his kilt. The only obvious thing Perry could see was missing - thankfully - was a set of bagpipes. He always understood that his uncle's taste knew no bounds, that there were no depths it would not plummet and right here, right now, was proof positive.

'I'm... I'm Sorry,' Perry overheard one of the brown attired guests announce to his uncle as he began his circuit around the room. Perry soon realised it was the motorcycle rider he had met earlier in the day. He thought he had recognised the smell of musty wallet and despair. Just to be sure, he pulled his hat down slightly to help offer more of a disguise.

'I'm sorry?' shrugged Uncle Hugo with a quizzical look upon his face, not understanding why the strange man had just apologised to him.

Uncle Hugo's hand quickly shot out and swooped a glass from Perry's tray. It reminded Perry of a toad's tongue darting out and capturing a fly. Following his lead, both guests standing with him also took a drink.

'No... No,' grumbled the guest who had just seemed to apologise. 'You are not Sorry, I am Sorry, Sorry Noakes to be exact. I'm staying here for the sales convention.'

Perry could tell by his expression that this was a routine he often went through with such a silly name. The pained look he sported was suddenly wiped from his face after a sip of the wine. Like battery acid his dad had once remarked.

'And Mr Noakes,' said Uncle Hugo unabated, 'what exactly is it that you are peddling if I may ask?'

'You... You may,' replied Sorry. His watery, manic eyes, stared at them through his thick spectacles. They flitted left and right as if constantly on the lookout for an escape route.

'Why... Why I sell socks. Socks of all makes, colours and sizes.'

'Oh really,' said Uncle Hugo, whose interest was piqued. Uncle Hugo liked socks, but in all fairness, he also liked tweed balaclavas.

Sorry Noakes bent over and attempted to raise both trouser legs over what looked like very muscular calves. This was not the case however, as it was soon revealed that Mr Noakes was wearing around twenty socks on each foot.

He began to hop on the spot as he rolled each pair down in turn - wool, nylon, cotton, plain, striped, polka dot, ankle, mid calf, knee high. On he continued in the most bizarre of sales pitches.

'I... I thank you for the purchase, Mr BUMbler,' said Sorry Noakes, once a deal was finally struck.

Both Uncle Hugo and Perry inwardly cringed.

'So... So, I will put you down for the three pairs of toe socks in various animal prints,' Sorry smiled.

His face soured again when he took another sip of his drink. 'Blimey,' he whistled.

Uncle Hugo turned to the second guest and raised his eyebrow in a command to speak, which they quickly seized.

'Hello there,' I'm Jimmy,' he crooned.

'Jimmy James,' he purred.

'Jimmy James Jr., he cooed in a velvety foreign tone. 'Can I just say I adore this tiny country of yours. It is just so small and sweet. This is my first time here on the international sales circuit.'

Perry would happily admit he was enthralled. Jimmy James Jr. was an American, easily as tall as any basketball player he had ever seen on TV. He displayed a golden tan and blue sparkling eyes. From what Perry could judge, he looked to be in his early twenties. He wore his blonde hair long, well past his shoulders with matching facial hair.

He was in a baggy ill fitting pastel blue suit with seriously enormous lapels. Perry took a moment to reflect on the danger young Jr. would be in if he were to venture outside in these high winds, he would take off like a paper aeroplane. Perry was disappointed to note that there were no cowboy boots on display, instead at the bottom of the flared trousers poked out a pair of open toed sandals. Perry also could not keep his eyes off the audacious belt buckle on display, which featuring a large, bejewelled letter 'J'.

'What are you selling?' gushed Perry.

Jimmy James Jr. placed his untouched drink back on Perry's tray, ignored him and continued speaking to Uncle Hugo in his melodic tone.

'It's a device I'm sure you will come to love and cherish as much as I have,' he said smoothly as he flicked his hair over his shoulder dramatically. 'It's a thing of beauty, a versatile eating instrument, with all the benefits of a spoon... plus a fork.... combined!' He then, as if by magic, whipped out an example from his sleeve, holding it aloft with pride.

'Interesting,' said Uncle Hugo, who was positively not interested.

'It's... It's a spork,' hissed Sorry Noakes, almost in disgust. He took another sip of wine and the look of disgust solidified.

'Hey,' said Jimmy James Jr., 'that's a scintillating name. Spork. SPORK. Is it taken?'

'Is... Is it taken? Is it taken!' Sorry's voice was growing shriller. 'It's a Spork! This is the laughingstock of the cutlery world! Despite being invented about 100 years ago, I thought everyone had seen the last of them back in the 1970's! Can I ask, did you just happen to find it in the pocket of that suit, when you procured it from the charity shop?' His face was getting redder. Perry thought it gave him a little character at least.

'Ah, not one like this though,' replied Jimmy James Jr. calmly. He then flashed a smile of unbridled whiteness, completely unnatural was its heavenly glow. 'This has been specifically designed. Look at the sleek shape. The aerodynamic curves and lines. Compared to boring cutlery like a dull spoon or plain fork, this little wonder just cuts through the air. The reduced drag on its way to and from the plate means you receive significantly more mouthfuls per minute. And what does that give you?'

'Let... Let me think, terminal indigestion?' retorted Sorry Noakes, who took a big swig of his drink and instantly regretted it. Again.

The snide remark just bounced off the jubilant entrepreneur, now lost in his own little infomercial. He worked the room with driven intensity.

'Why my friends, it gives you TIME. Time equates to FREEDOM. Freedom means more CHOICES. Choices enables REFLECTION and SELF-EXAMINATION. Once you stand up from that table and the mindless drones are still labouring away, you can head off and seize the day and change your life,' he chuckled to himself serenely.

'I can't quite pinpoint your accent,' said Uncle Hugo. Perry watched him as he eyed up the cheap suit on display, he was clearly not a fan. 'Assuming you are not a Canadian, from where in the America's do you hail?'

'Why Sir, I'm from California,' he uttered in pride.

'Ah, the City of Angels, Hollywood. Alas my travelling has not taken me there, yet. It is certainly on my list. Unfortunately, I have family commitments that tie me here. A dullard of a brother and his simple son. Workshy creatures both. They would be completely lost without me. No doubt they would both be living in a ditch within a week without my guiding hand. They are such a ball and chain. Fear not however, as I have recently found a bolt cutter and I will soon be free, have no worries on that score.'

Perry took that moment to storm off, but he could feel his uncle's mocking eyes burning into the back of his head as his own started to sting with tears.

Just to let know, as there are no secrets between us, if I am feeling a little saucy of an evening, I will wear a pair of sock suspenders. Just let that sink in. On another note, what a pair of gnashers that tall, long haired, flower child has. When he opens his mouth, it is like a lighthouse on a stormy night. Keep away and stay safe. I shall admit to a little jealousy on my part. My teeth can in no way be compared to his, but then, I do perform my own dentistry. Hence why I always wear a scarf over my face, to protect the innocent. HB

Chapter 14

Perry headed over towards his father, who was engaged in conversation with a short, stout woman. A sprinkling of freckles covered her pale skin, as if they were the only one's brave enough to have made an appearance. There was something about her bearing that made Perry want to offer a salute and shout *ma'am, yes ma'am.*

She looked to be in her late thirties and was wearing a smart lavender tweed jacket with matching skirt down to her ankles. Her wild ginger curly hair was being held in place with copious amounts of hair pins. Perry bet she could set off an airport alarm at one hundred yards.

The patio doors suddenly rattled. The weather outside was getting worse, the wind and rain were now battering hard against every side the hotel had to offer. It was at this moment that Perry realised all the lights in the room had now been switched on. Despite it being only lunchtime, the drawing room would have been shrouded in darkness otherwise.

'Can I interest you in a drink,' his father asked. She turned and swiped one from the tray without so much as a thank you. Perry looked at his dad and then looked at the tray. His father almost panicked.

'Oh no, not for me, I'm working. Perry, can I introduce you to Ms Harrumph.'

'Philippa, this is my son Perry.'

Ms Harrumph's face curdled. Perry was not sure if it was due to the drink or the introduction.

'OOOF, THAT WILL PUT HAIRS ON YOUR CHEST,' she bellowed.

Perry was surprised that so small a mouth could emit such an expressive noise. It was all rambunctious and foghorn like in its manner.

'Er... yes, my brother Hugo procures it from a small manufacturer, all locally sourced.'

Perry guessed this was technically the truth, you couldn't get more local that the hotel itself.

'So, Philippa, am I correct in saying you are also here for the sales gathering nearby?'

'I AM INDEED,' she cried. She took another big gulp of the drink, finished it and took another from Perry's lofted tray. He was impressed. As was his father.

'What is it that you specialise in?' he prompted after no more information was forthcoming.

'FUDGE,' she almost screamed, which made Perry jump.

'Fudge,' repeated his dad, far quieter.

'WHY HAVE SWEET FUDGE. WHEN YOU CAN ALSO HAVE THE SOUR,' she boomed.

'FUDGE SO BITTER. IT WILL MAKE YOUR FACE COLLAPSE IN ON ITSELF,' she roared.

'FUDGE SALTIER THAN ALL THE SEVEN SEA'S I HAVE SAILED,' she wailed.

'GLITTERY FUDGE. THAT SPARKLES AND SHIMMERS WHEN IT GOES IN... AND SHINES AND TWINKLES ON THE WAY OUT,' she hollered.

'SPICY FUDGE. THAT WILL SHOOT STEAM OUT OF YOUR EARS. IT WILL SWEAT THE SHOES OFF YOUR FEET. YOU WOULD ONLY EAT IT IN THE ANTARTIC,' she yelled.

'I SELL SMOOTH FUDGE. LUMPY FUDGE. GLOW IN THE DARK FUDGE. FUDGE AS LIGHT AS AIR. FUDGE THAT WILL CURL YOUR HAIR. A FUDGE SO UNLIKE FUDGE I LEGALLY CAN'T CALL IT FUDGE,' she growled.

'YES, FUDGE MAKES THE WORLD GO ROUND AND SOON I WILL BE PROMOTING OUR NEWEST OFFERING, WE CALL IT... CHUDGE!'

'Chudge,' repeated his father, who absentmindedly rubbed his ringing ear and then checked his finger to make sure there was no blood.

'YES, CHEESY FUDGE!'

'Very interesting,' he managed to mutter back, before swiping a glass from Perry's tray and taking a large swallow. He needed the succour.

'IT WAS MY LATE FATHER'S BUSINESS,' Ms Harrumph continued as she took a third glass from Perry's now almost depleted tray.

'I'm sorry to hear that.'

'HE DIED OF CHaFBYS.'

'CHaFBYS, I... I don't think I've ever heard of that. Is it some form of disease?'

Perry found himself taking a step back just to be safe.

'IF YOU HAPPEN TO COUGH - HICCUP AND FART - BURB - YAWN - SNEEZE, ALL AT THE SAME MOMENT, ALL AT THE SAME TIME... INSTANT DEATH. THE BODY JUST SHUTS DOWN. IT'S HIGHLY RARE.'

'It's... highly unusual I must admit,' offered his dad.

Highly improbable was what Perry was thinking.

'Ms Harrumph, I hope you don't mind me asking, but have you spent any time in the forces?'

'WHY YES,' she snapped to attention, her back ramrod straight, 'I'M SURPRISED YOU NOTICED. I WAS IN THE NAVY FOR MANY YEARS BEFORE I WAS FORCED TO RETIRE. THERE WE WERE. DRIFTING IN ENEMY WATERS. WE COULDN'T SEE THEM. BUT THEY COULD SEE US. IT

WAS A STROKE OF LUCK TO BE SURE. A TORPEDO. IT WOULD HAVE SUNK THE SHIP. ALL HANDS LOST. WE THINK IT RICHOCHETTED OFF A DOLPHIN. IT LANDED UP ON THE DECK. THERE IT WAS. TICKING AWAY. THE WHOLE CREW FROZE. I MOVED. I ACTED. I HAD TO SAVE THE SHIP. I RAN TOWARDS IT. GAVE IT AN ALMIGHTY KICK. THERE WAS AN EXPLOSION. PAIN. I BLACKED OUT. I SAVED THE SHIP. BUT MY TIME IN THE NAVY CAME TO AN END.

'It blew your leg off didn't it! Is it wooden? Can you show me,' said Perry excitedly.

His father's eyebrows almost shot off his face.

'WHAAAT! NO. I KICKED IT OFF THE SHIP. IT WENT OFF HARMLESSLY. IN DEEP WATER. I BROKE ALL THE TOES ON MY FOOT HOWEVER. THEY HAVE NEVER HEALED PROPERLY. THEY ALWAYS THROB WHEN I'M NEAR THE WATER. NO MORE SAILING AND SHIPS FOR ME.'

'The Navy's loss is the fudge worlds gain I guess,' said his father, ever the diplomat. As Ms Harrumph took another swig of her drink, he cast Perry a dirty look and signalled for him to move on, which Perry duly did.

There was one last full glass on his tray, so he moved over to the elderly man who was sitting alone. He was wearing a funeral black suit, as if he had been buried in it, but instead of a tie it was a cravat that sprouted out of his open necked shirt. At first glance he had looked asleep, but as Perry got nearer, he could see his watery grey eyes darting about.

'Hello there,' he said looking up, 'what's your name?'

'It's Perry sir, would you like a glass of wine?'

'Heavens no,' he replied, 'I have been watching the rather pained expressions on everyone's face, so I think I will pass on that, if you don't mind.'

'A wise choice,' said Perry who was warming to the elderly man.

'Sorry for my rudeness, I'm Gentle-Me, Seymour Gentle-Me and can I just say I do like your uniform.'

'You do?' said Perry in surprise.

'Absolutely not,' he laughed. 'What on Earth was your uncle thinking of? I'm assuming it was all his idea. He was dressed like he was playing a round of crazy golf this morning. And now... well please tell me that costume doesn't come equipped with bagpipes does it! He's not going to play a little ditty for us as we head off for lunch!'

'I certainly hope not, but I can't be 100% sure.'

'One can but hope lad. If he does come see me, I have some croutons on me, very versatile, you can even ram them in your ears. I did it earlier to try and drown out that awful shouty woman. Anyway, I have to say I've been in many, many hotels in my time and your uncle certainly has some strange ideas on how to run one.'

Then it happened. In a flash. A flash of lightning that was. It briefly lit the outside of the hotel as if it were morning and in exchange the inside fell into complete inky blackness.

My, she seemed like a force of nature. I certainly would not like to get on the wrong side of her. I was deeply sorry to hear about her father. My record was a simultaneous sneeze/belch/fart. I was quite proud at the time to be honest, never realised I was toying with potential death, however. HB

Chapter 15

'**Eeeek..,**' came a high-pitched whistling squeal from somewhere in the darkened room.

Somehow Perry could instantly tell it was Sorry Noakes. There then followed a cacophony of shouting from the others.

'OUTRAGEOUS! WHO TOUCHED MY...'

'Wow, did someone forget to pay the utility bill...'

'**Eeeek...**'

'Will you stop shrieking like a teenage girl, my poor ears...'

It was the power; they had lost the power to the lights. Although the room was in a blanket of gloom you could just make out people and objects, but light was much needed, and not just the haunting luminosity provided by the teeth of Jimmy James Jr.

'Don't worry everyone,' said Perry's father, taking command of the situation. 'I will secure some candles and be straight back. Grubbins, if you don't mind.'

And with that the dim figures of his father and the bartender strode out of the drawing room. Perry could just make out Ms Harrumph rummaging around in her bag and then to his amazement...

'I KNEW I HAD IT HERE SOMEWHERE,' she proclaimed as she waved a small lump of glowing fudge before her like a radioactive nugget.

Everyone stood still in the darkness with only the fury of the weather outside filling the empty void.

'Gee whiz, it sounds bad out there. Back home there are tornados that can carry off a building or flatten a house. Do you get much of that over here?' asked Jimmy James Jr.

'WHAAAT!' erupted the powerful voice of Ms Harrumph. 'OUTSIDE IS NOTHING MORE THAN A LITTLE STORM. THIS IS A STURDY HOTEL THAT HAS SUFFERED NOUGHT BUT AN INCONVENIENT POWER CUT, NOTHING MORE, NOTHING LESS.'

Soon glowing candles appeared at the entrance to the drawing room as his dad and Grubbins returned.

'Never fear,' piped up the voice of Uncle Hugo. 'Silly weather, I'm sure the power will be restored shortly, but in the meantime, these can light our way.' He started to place the newly lit candles around the room.

Perry watched as his father and Grubbins both set off again to do the same in reception and throughout other parts of the hotel.

Uncle Hugo was in the middle of placing a candle on the mantlepiece when 'flashpoint', as it was later to be named began. A horrendous roar of thunder from outside was accompanied by a gale of epic proportions that forced the patio doors to burst open. It was bedlam.

Many of the newly placed candles were snuffed out in an instance as the gusty wind blew into the hotel. Alarmingly, it caught the wispy grey hair of Mr Gentle-Me, who was sat in his chair open mouthed.

'Oh my....,' he managed to mutter before his hair piece began to levitate in the air, much to the amazement of everyone who could still see. The invisible string holding it mid air was finally cut and it was unceremoniously dumped onto the ground. It looked like a rat after an unfortunate incident with a steamroller. Mr Gentle-Me's bald pink pate was also now left open to the elements.

'Oh my...,' he managed to wheeze again.

Perry fought against the constricting tightness of his suit as he rushed to close the wide-open patio doors. Wind, rain, leaves, branches, it was all pouring into the room at horrendous speed.

Another fierce, foul draught burst into the hotel, although a ratty looking wig was the least of its targets. It was a moment that would never be erased from the memory, despite attempts at expensive therapy and radical hypnosis. It was the horrifying imagery of Uncle Hugo's kilt, flying up about him as he stood there, trying to shield his flickering candle.

'The doors you idiot boy, the doors,' roared Uncle Hugo as he jigged on the spot, which if anything made the resulting scene even more sickening.

No one was paying any attention to the patio doors, even Perry if truth be told. Everyone had forgotten all about poor Mr Gentle-Me and the revelation of his sad toupee and bald head. There was a new sight in town ladies and gentlemen, one to scar the mind - the unholy view of white, fleshy, pasty, dancing buttocks that Uncle Hugo was now exposing.

CENSORED

Unfortunately, nobody got a better view of them than poor Mr Gentle-Me. It was ill timing to be sure, for Mr Gentle-Me had just bent from his chair to reclaim his wig and now his face was but inches away from the ghastly mooning hotelier.

'**My... My eyes**...,' screamed Sorry Noakes who began theatrically staggering about with his hands over his face. He got as far as one of the small tables before crashing over it on to the floor in a heap.

'WHAAAT! PUT IT AWAY MAN. SEVENTEEN YEARS IN THE NAVY AND I'VE NEVER HAD TO ENDURE ANYTHING QUITE LIKE THIS!'

'Zowie! I must admit this was not something I was expecting to see on my travels. A true Scotsman. Just wait till my folks get the postcard about this.'

The kilt, much to the fury of Uncle Hugo, and the terror of everyone else, continued to fiercely flutter and thrash up around him, despite his best attempts to keep it under control.

'The doors you stupid boy, close the blasted doors,' his purple faced uncle screamed, in his losing battle to protect his modesty and keep the candle lit.

Snapping out of his trance, Perry began wrestling against the force of the tempest and the mechanics of the handles, finally managing to get the doors closed and properly locked.

At once the billowing kilt slowly dropped, ending the ordeal for all.

As quickly as it had begun, the pandemonium ceased and the room fell into an appreciative, if not awkward silence. But as we know, nature abhors a vacuum.

'WHAAAT! WAS THAT A TATTOO OF A WAFFLE ON HIS BOTTOM?' announced Ms Harrumph, in one of the loudest whispers heard in years.

'It... It looked like a hashmark to me,' offered Sorry Noakes.

'I hope so, I would have sworn it was a hamster cage, and I hate animal cruelty,' added Jimmy Jones Jr.

Uncle Hugo slowly turned around, his sweaty face burning brightly enough to have made the candle he saved almost redundant. Farcically, everyone quickly looked away as if nothing of note had happened.

Everyone that was except for a very shocked Mr Gentle-Me. He sat there, frozen in place, his arm outstretched but his wig long forgotten, staring up at Uncle Hugo. Perry could not be sure but the look of shock on his wrinkly face was turning into one of confusion.

What Perry did not notice however, was that Uncle Hugo had read the expression on Mr Gentle-Me's face and the one he left in return was dark indeed.

I felt so sorry for them. Luckily, I knew what was about to happen, so I was prepared. I steeled myself for the horror that was about to unfold. But let this be a lesson to all of you. No matter how young or old, underwear is essential. Needless to say, the cleaner the better. HB

Chapter 16

'It's all very quiet in here,' said Perry's father as he walked back into the drawing room. He noticed that some of the candles were now out and began relighting them.

'Yes, well... err...,' struggled Uncle Hugo, still overcome with shame.

'Belinda tells me lunch is ready, do you want to get everyone over?'

'Yes, yes,' uttered Uncle Hugo, desperate to put events behind him, so to speak. 'Everyone, everyone, lunch is now served, if you could please just follow my brother Erstwhile, thank you.'

Soon enough they were all steered back across reception towards the dining room. Everyone began taking their seats at the large mahogany table, now fully lit with a collection of ornate candelabras. It lent itself a rather atmospheric occasion. One could almost have forgotten it was because they were in the middle of a power cut. Uncle Hugo, sitting at the head of the table, addressed his audience.

'I shall admit that the jewel in the crown of this hotel is none other than our very own cook Belinda. I swear she could make a five-course meal with nothing but a candle and a tin of beans. I suppose if this blackout continues, she may well be forced to.'

He chuckled at his own little joke, the smug irritating Uncle Hugo of old was now returning.

'In fact, I think if I was to ever get rid of this hotel, I would still have to retain her services as my personal chef,' and with that he turned to Perry, who was standing in the corner of the room and gave him a sly wink.

He knows! Perry's blood turned cold. His legs felt like jelly. Uncle Hugo KNEW that he was on to him. Aware of the fact he had seen the documents. And what was worse - he did not seem to care. The situation was spiralling out of control, perhaps he was too late to save the hotel and his parents' marriage.

'If you could all join me in a round of applause, as I present to you our very own Belinda,' continued Uncle Hugo.

There followed a muted round of handclapping from the unenthused guests. Belinda then strode out of the kitchen.

She was at least in her sixties, with a huge mop of curly hair. A huge mop of curly hair flourished in a very unnatural colour. *Coal Miner Black* if Perry had to guess, but he knew one thing for sure, he was never going to ask her. Malaika had once joked that the Plimsoll Bandit may have hidden the crown jewels in Belinda's unruly locks. He was forced to admit it would have been a wonderful hiding place and they would have remained missing forever, as no one would have been brave enough to attempt a rescue.

Belinda herself was a squat, thick set woman, compact and powerful like a coiled spring. Very imposing in a wide and solid way. It may have been true that Ms Harrumph gave off a military vibe, but with Belinda it was the threat of imminent violence. She had the lumbering motion of a heavyweight wrestler, just waiting to suplex you off a kitchen counter.

'Now Belinda, what delights do you have in store for us?' said Uncle Hugo, drawing out the whole pantomime.

'Sprouts,' she grunted.

'Ha,' gushed Uncle Hugo. 'What she means is that we are about to enjoy a celebration, nay, a homage to the glory of the humble Brussels Sprouts. A celebrated tradition built into the historical fabric of this tiny part of the world.'

So, thought Perry to himself, that is what was in the two mysterious sacks delivered the day before. With his uncle personally involved in the transaction, they had no doubt *fallen off the back of a lorry* or were well past their best, assuming sprouts even have a best. It had potentially been both options and he was getting them for a ridiculously cheap price. He could think of no other reason. True, they used to be grown around these parts, many years ago, but everyone hated them and there was certainly no tradition that would welcome them back to anyone's table. Good luck to him if he thinks he can pull this trick off at dinner as well, there would be a riot.

'I promise you all a sprout spectacular. We have superior sprout soup, followed by succulent sprout pizza or scrumptious sprout burger, if you so desire, all washed down with splendid spicy sprout smoothies. Last, but certainly not least, we have a local delicacy - sticky sweet and salted sprout scones submerged in a sprout sorbet.' Uncle Hugo, who was well and truly flogging a dead horse, thankfully finished speaking.

The hotel guests sat in a state of apathetic disappointment. If tumbleweed had rolled across the dining room table, Perry would not have been surprised. It would have been more nutritious as well.

'You have surpassed yourself again Belinda,' Uncle Hugo cheered.

'I'm a little rusty,' she croaked, as she smashed her thick ham like fist into the palm of the other. The intention was clear. Perry hoped no one would be half-witted enough to be critical in her presence.

Grubbins soon appeared, his tray laden with bowls of sprout soup, which were soon shared amongst everyone. Belinda retreated to her lair.

'Bon Appétit,' shouted Uncle Hugo, who began slurping from his bowl noisily.

My... My soup is cold, stone cold,' complained Sorry Noakes. He looked down at his bowl suspiciously, the sprouts were suspended in a thin looking grey gruel, they bobbed about like dead bodies floating on the tide.

'I believe it is a 'Gazpacho', it is meant to be served cold,' advised Mr Gentle-Me, who pushed his own bowl as far away from himself as possible.

I would not be so sure about that, thought Perry to himself, who had suffered the same fate many times in the past.

'WHAAAT! WHY ARE YOU ARE SERVING US THESE VEGAN GRENADES. HAVE YOU TAKEN LEAVE OF YOUR SENSES? YOU HAVE OBVIOUSLY NEVER SPENT

PROLONGED TIME IN CLOSE PROXIMITY WITH OTHERS,' warned Ms Harrumph.

Jimmy James Jr. however was delighted.

'Thank you, this looks lovely. I find nothing augments my spiritual connection to the Earth more than eating the bountiful offerings it supplies,' he sang. He swooped up a sprout on his spoon and munched on it contentedly. 'Zooey Mamma,' he shrieked, jumping to his feet while clutching his mouth.

'Anything wrong down there,' muttered Uncle Hugo, who did not even look up from his bowl and continued to slurp loudly.

'I... I... think I have chipped a tooth.'

'On a sprout?' laughed Uncle Hugo.

Jimmy James Jr. lifted one from his bowl, held it aloft and dropped it. The sprout clattered onto the table like a brick.

'Corr... Corr Blimey,' uttered Sorry Noakes, who eyed his own bowl with even greater suspicion.

Despite the sinking feeling in the pit of his stomach, from Uncle Hugo's previous taunt, Perry had a job to do. He moved around the table lifting bowls, replacing cutlery and with the help of Grubbins brought out the rest of the sprout themed dishes, one devastating creation after the other. The table was understandably low on conversation, heads were down as they tried to make the best out of an unpleasant situation. Belinda had truly made them tap out.

Still, everyone had managed to eat a little of something, that was except for Mr Gentle-Me, who had only played with his food. He seemed to have lost a little colour after the experience in the drawing room, a quizzical expression now etched on his face. For once none of this could be blamed on Belinda's cooking. Perry also noticed Mr Gentle-Me's hairpiece was sitting just as lopsided as his hat. When he next passed him, Perry vowed to try and knock the wig back into alignment.

With the guests partially fed and all the doors and windows firmly locked to avoid any further unpleasantries, lunch had at least been conducted civilly, if not successfully. Perry's thoughts on his own situation had stewed over the period and he had decided he was no longer going to take any more of his uncle's behaviour; enough was enough. It would soon be time to take matters into his own hands. In fact, today's events might make things a little easier. The disturbance to the usual pattern of the day and lack of light, may just give him an extra ounce of good luck, which he would need if the key were to be his.

Uncle Hugo, his kilt stretched tightly across his expanded stomach, grunted as he fought to stand up and make an announcement.

'Now, usually after a little lunch I would recommend nothing better than a walk around the lovely hotel grounds. Alas, I would certainly not suggest that today.' To further back up his comment the thunderous rain could be heard from outside.

'As many of you have just arrived from your travels, perhaps it is best if you seize this opportunity to have a little rest. A multitude of candles have been placed throughout the hotel, so we can at least all see where we are going. We will also give you some to take back to your rooms.' There was a general murmur of agreement from the table.

'The drawing room will remain open however, should you wish to pop down later for a little pre dinner drink. The dinner gong will be rung at 6pm precisely, please enjoy your continued stay and I shall update you as soon as we hear anything further on the power situation. My apologies again.'

The guests slowly raised themselves from their seats and one by one they trapsed up to their rooms, waving their flickering candles before them to light the way. Perry thought it all looked very surreal.

He then helped Grubbins clear the table and tidy the room, as his father headed off to staff the reception desk. Uncle Hugo, who once again was avoiding any work, was no doubt sloping off upstairs to pick another ridiculous outfit for later in the day. He did pause at the doorway however, turned, and gave Perry a sneering smile that drove a shudder up his nephew's spine.

That sounded like a right good nosh up considering the circumstances. Then again, I have just finished a course of dried herring on digestive biscuit, a blue cheese and raison frittata, all wrapped up with a big bowl of curdled custard with diced banana peel. I will admit I may not be the best person to pass judgement. HB

Chapter 17

With the guests out of the way and his father and uncle occupied, it only left Grubbins, Belinda and himself to clean, tidy and prepare for later in the day.

Perry had a deep fondness for Grubbins, he kept to himself and was a hard worker to boot. That said, the one small thing that irked him, was that Uncle Hugo gave Grubbins very wide latitude when it came to his attire. Today for example, while Perry was dressed as if he was off to a fancy dress party, Grubbins was wearing a simple black t-shirt. Nothing wrong with that you would think, until you realise it was at least several sizes too small. At a certain angle you could be mistaken for thinking it had been painted on. If that was not bad enough, the short, overly tight t-shirt, always hung tantalizingly above his naval, just failing to cover the abnormal belly button he sported.

Perhaps abnormal was slightly harsh, but it had always given Perry cause for concern. Most people have a belly button like a little cave, where during the night tiny fairies made their beds. That little piece of fluff you always manage to dig out - that was once their pillow. Well, that's what his mum had always told him, and he believed it. In fact, for the last few years, he had always put some tape over his before going to bed.

Some special people do not have to worry about that, as their belly button was classed as an 'outie', shaped like a little nubbin. In Grubbins case he had taken things to an extreme. His was not an outie. His was a super outie. His outie belly button was like a miniature Ben Nevis. Yes, the big mountain. Which, ironically enough, is shaped identically like Grubbins belly button, but slightly bigger.

'So Grubbins, once this place is cleared what are you getting up to next?' asked Perry.

'Well, I don't expect anyone to be rushing downstairs again, after all the food that was served, so I was going to head off to the office and gather my thoughts. I'll pop back to the bar in half an hour or so.' He absently toyed with his fluffy sideburns.

'Cool,' Perry replied. That was exactly what he wanted to hear for his plan to have any success. He grabbed the last tottering pile of dirty dishes and carefully made his way into the hotel kitchen, the domain of Belinda.

When he was younger, Perry had mistakenly thought that Grubbins and Belinda were married to each other and then that they were brother and sister. He was wrong on both counts, they were simply two very strange individuals, whom fate had decreed would work together at the High Hill Hotel. As far as he was concerned, they were part of his family now.

He stopped again to think about the future, his own, his parents, and if they did not reclaim the hotel, Grubbins and Belinda as well. It truly pained Perry to think of the damage his uncle would inflict on everyone if he did manage to sell up. This helped to steel himself for what was needed next. He simply had to secure the key to the catacombs.

It was a place that had never interested him before, no doubt dark, dank, dusty, and filled with spiders. No thank you. As a rule, it was somewhere that only Grubbins really dared to go, he knew for a fact his uncle would not go down there for all the suits on Saville Row.

'Will you stop daydreaming boy,' came a voice from the darkened kitchen. Belinda walked over to him and grabbed the plates from his grasp. He had thought them heavy, but they were nothing to her. 'I have enough on my hands without you dawdling about.'

Belinda, although she hid it well, had a heart of gold. She was originally hired as a security consultant of all things. This was back in the day when Uncle Hugo used to panic every time he received a little hate mail. Complaints, and the odd threat, from previous guests who took a dislike to his toxic attitude. So, for a period, she was his bodyguard.

When Uncle Hugo became hardened to the criticism and it became clear nothing was ever going to happen to him, he decided to install her as the hotel's new cook. It was partly a penny-pinching exercise, as she had zero experience, and partly because the previous incumbent had stormed out after refusing to cook a rabbit for dinner that Uncle Hugo had found by the side of the road. At least some people still had standards.

Needless to say, it had been a rollercoaster of a ride ever since. Uncle Hugo had learned that the trick was to introduce Belinda to her intended victims in advance. When everyone was aware of exactly what they would be dealing with, there were no complaints, just a lot of suffering in silence. Their words would shrivel up and die in their mouths, just as the food had done in Belinda's oven. Worse case scenario, it would be a strongly worded letter sent from the safety of their own home, with no return address, just before they left the country for a spell.

Perry did remember one poor soul, who objected to finding a used plaster in his mash. Belinda, all smiles, had apologised profusely and insisted on giving him a tour of the kitchen to put his mind at rest. Tripped over his own shoelaces was the official verdict and he sat there quivering, eager to sign the accident report. It still did not quite explain his black eye or account for the sheer amount of mash that had ended up each nostril. But these things happen it seems. Perry had quickly learned that the following adage should always be followed; you do not trifle with Belinda, nor go near any trifle from Belinda.

The most amazing thing was that Uncle Hugo continued to keep her on. Each mealtime was a trip into uncharted territory. You started with a solid belief it would not end well and rarely were you ever disappointed. Perry put a lot of it down to the fact that Uncle Hugo, somehow, seemed to like her food. He certainly never suffered any ill effects, which was more than could be said for most guests. One day, if he was generous enough to donate his body to medical science, these and many more questions could finally be answered.

Like Grubbins, she dressed as she pleased, which usually took the form of slippers, wrinkly tights, floral dresses, and aprons, the gaudier the better. They looked as if they had been recycled from curtains of a bygone era.

Trying to get a feel for Belinda's mood was also notoriously difficult, in the main due to the thick layers of makeup she trowelled onto her face. She was all blue eye shadow with rosy, pink checks, bookending a pair of thin lips coated with industrial strength lipstick. One kiss from those, should she be so inclined, and you had a better chance of washing off a tattoo.

'You are up to something boy, I can tell, out with it.'

'Me, eh, no,' gasped Perry. She was a terrible cook but was brilliant at detecting potential mischief.

'Well, if I catch you up to anything...,' she let the threat hang in the air as she flexed her bicep.

Perry looked her straight in her overly large right eye. 'I'm not up to anything Belinda, honest. It's just this uniform, it's quite tight and scratchy around the collar, plus I'm a bit scared with the hotel being all dark, and of course earlier Uncle Hugo flashed his...'

'Okay, okay, the less I hear about that the better.'

'Are you going to be okay for dinner, what with the power cut?'

'I'll be fine boy; the gas is still working, and I have enough light to get by. I'm busy though, so if you don't mind, out of my kitchen.'

Perry did not need to be told twice. He would now have free reign of the hotel for about the next thirty minutes, which should be more than enough time. Grab the key, find the treasure with Malaika tomorrow, save the hotel and all will be well. Now it was time for Project Liberate...

Now, I know people have climbed it. Ben Nevis that is, not Grubbins belly button. Although I am prone to believe it could be possible, if you had a mind to and if he allowed it. I wonder if anyone has asked? The fact that he likes to show it off every day with his tight-fitting t-shirts makes you think he is flaunting it. Perhaps hoping a would-be mountaineer would dare to attempt it. As hard as I have looked, I could not see any snowy peaks upon it, or more importantly a flag to indicate that it had been conquered.

This Belinda. They say everyone has a double, but could it be her? The one they called the 'Mooneye'. Last seen in the Malaysian fighting pits. A supreme and brutal fighter feared and unbeaten. Just to make it clear I am not going to ask her. HB

Chapter 18

On his run through the driving rain back to the hotel, Perry had been thinking and formulating. How to get the key from Grubbins that could save the day. He could of course just tell him the truth, perhaps Grubbins would just give him it, maybe even help. Perry didn't want to leave it to chance however, he couldn't risk Grubbins saying anything to his father, or worse, Uncle Hugo. No, he had to find a way to sneak it from him undetected.

A rough scheme started to shape in his mind and a fun filled day that Malaika and he had once shared at the hotel would prove to be pivotal to his plan...

Let everything shimmer as we again go back in time... HB.

'It's... it's... magnificent!' Malaika took stuttering steps into the large bright room not quite believing what her eyes were telling her.

'Oh really,' replied Perry, 'I thought you would have gone with... over the top, or self indulgent, maybe a plain old, this is ridiculous.'

'Ssssh...,' went Malaika, her eyes as wide as they could possibly be.

'So, it's actually two old guest rooms knocked together, Uncle Hugo had a wall taken away. We are now probably standing in the biggest walk-in wardrobe in the whole country.'

'It's... it's... amazing,' was all that Malaika could offer.

What they had just stumbled into was a labyrinth of clothes racks. Row upon row. Line after line. All leading this way and that. If there was order to this chaos, then they both could not work it out. All the hangers were overflowing with daywear, nightwear, sportswear, and fancy dress. A winding maze of jackets and trousers, suits, shirts, and coats. Hat boxes stood tottering till they almost reached the ceiling. Shoe boxes took up one side of an entire wall. The place was awash with sensational colour and splendour. It was simply... mind blowing.

'I like to sneak in here when my uncle is away on his frequent holidays, just to try stuff on.' He had no idea if Malaika had heard him, she seemed spellbound. 'As long as we put everything back where we found it, we will be fine. It looks like utter disorder but I'm sure he has some system. Let's do it.'

'Do what?' muttered Malaika her brain near overloading.

'Let's try some clothes on, right now.'

Malaika certainly heard that, as a great smile broke out on her face, and she was off running down an overflowing aisle of swimsuits.

Perry returned to the agreed meeting spot, wearing an oversized pair of black trousers, with black suspenders draped over a black and white striped t-shirt. Atop his head sat a black beret, a red scarf was tied around his neck, and he wore a pair of white gloves. He stood there silently...

'What are you wearing?' asked Malaika, slightly confused.

Perry ignored her and began placing his hands flat out before him, to the side of him, above him. He was trapped in an invisible box.

Malaika gave him a mighty kick in the shin.

'Aaaarrgh...,' screamed Perry, the silence broken as he jumped up and down clutching his freshly bruised leg.

'I hate mime artists,' she said as way of justification, rather than apology.

She herself had been transformed into a 70's disco icon. Massive star shaped shades covered her face, which was in shadow from the large silver sequined flat cap she was wearing. A super feathery yellow boa was draped around her shoulders, and she had donned a pair of neon green dungarees. The crowning glory was the hefty looking mirrored roller skates on her feet.

'No wonder that hurt,' laughed Perry who was still rubbing his shin. 'You win this round,' and he quickly hobbled off down the clothing corridor for something else.

And on it went...

Soon Perry was standing there in a giant pair of green waders, a waterproof vest covered in pockets and a wide brimmed hat adorned with a multitude of colourful fly-fishing hooks. He erratically waved an antique looking fishing rod over his head as if he was about to cast off.

'Excuse me Miss, would you like to accompany me on my rowing boat down the Didwob river. I'm off to catch a fish or two for tea. The boat has a slow leak however, so there is a small chance we may need to swim back.'

'That's a no from me,' thundered Malaika, who waddled from around a corner. She was hidden somewhere inside a partially inflated sumo wrestler suit. 'I'm far too busy training for my next fight,' she squatted and stomped her feet menacingly causing Perry to turn and run off before he was attacked again.

And on it continued...

A flashy highly polished pair of shoes made an appearance, quickly followed by the rest of Perry. He performed a rather ornate tap dance routine, completely muffled by the carpet, as he slowly made his way into the centre of the room. He had pulled on a black top hat and tailcoat, and with his cane twirling by his side he was the very dapper picture of sophistication.

Malaika couldn't help herself and burst out laughing, but all Perry could do was stare back at her slack jawed and open mouthed. She looked stunning, standing there in a shimmering golden ballgown.

'I don't mean to be funny, but why does your uncle have this?'

'Can I have this dance,' Perry whispered, summoning up the courage to ask and completely ignoring the valid point Malaika had just made. For the next few minutes, they were lost to their own internal music as they twisted and turned around the room, skipping, swaying, and whirling up and down the lines of clothing.

And on it resumed...

The next hour was a blur of fun and frolics in this Aladdin's cave of fashion faux pas, appalling apparel, silly suits, grotesque garments, and odious outfits.

And we are back again, more glitter everyone... HB.

It had been one of the best, most cherished days Perry had enjoyed in the hotel for a long, long time.

But that was then, and this was now, and little did Perry realise just how important that day would be in helping him fulfil his cunning plan.

I am a man of simple tastes. I wear an overcoat, collar turned up. A fedora hat and a scarf. I wear it on the streets of capital cities. I wear it on the beach. Whilst traversing the North Pole or scouring around the Amazon. It is my signature look, my unique selling point, my uniform. It is the essence of who I am. This Hugo person is still searching for who he is. This wardrobe, this constant changing of clothes and identities is a smokescreen. He is lost in life and just wants to find himself. I am sorry, that got a little deeper than I intended. I have been listening to those self help podcasts again. HB

Chapter 19

Perry was sitting in silence within the dining room with only the flickering candles for company. He looked at his watch; it had now been 10 minutes since Grubbins headed to his office. He could hear the dim clattering of Belinda, hard at work in the kitchen. It was time to make his move.

First, he had to head up to his room and collect the equipment he had stashed earlier, it would be needed if his efforts were to succeed. As he snuck back downstairs, he realised this wasn't a plan, it was a wing and a prayer. Perry had a terrible sinking feeling in his stomach that all he was going to do was deeply embarrass himself.

When he reached the ground floor he headed towards the corridor, where Grubbins had claimed a small, secluded room many years ago. It was his little bolt hole, his man cave, his tranquil island of solitude on the turbulent sea that was the High Hill Hotel. This is where he would come during any periods of down time, to ponder life and its mysteries, to read the paper, listen to cricket on the radio or to practice how long he could keep his eyes closed for.

Perry kicked off his shoes before he began his approach as they were traitorous and would no doubt start to squeak at the most inopportune time. Once he had walked around the village with Malaika and at least three cats had appeared, no doubt thinking a party of mice were on the loose.

Thankfully, the closer that Perry got to his target, he could hear the noise of grunting snoring trickling down the hall. So far, so good.

Perry quickly stuck his head into the room. Despite its small size it was still sparse, with only the odd cricketing picture stuck to the walls (a game his father hated with a passion) and a rather thirsty looking rubber plant in the corner. An antique looking radio, thick with dust, was gently playing some jazz music.

Grubbins was fast asleep on his chair, his feet up on the desk. A copy of the Little Didwob Gazette covered his face, the pages gently blowing up and down in time with his snoring. Then he saw them, the thick bunch of keys, hanging by a peg on the wall as he had expected. Perry then realised how fortunate he was and how fragile his so-called plan really was. What if the keys had still been attached to Grubbins belt. Perry cursed himself for this silly oversight, hopefully there wasn't anything else he had not accounted for, as he felt he had just used up all his luck.

Grubbins was positioned between him and the keys he needed; he may have been able to tiptoe up to him, but he still wouldn't have been close enough to grab them from the wall. Perry was prepared, however. He gently placed the top hat he had liberated earlier, from his uncle's walk-in wardrobe, onto the floor. Beneath it, tied with copious amounts of string, was one mirrored roller skate. He eyed up the distance, moved the hat slightly to the left with his foot, then slid it into the room with a kick. And what a kick it was. A deft little punt that saw the top hat slowly roll across the floor, under the chair Grubbins was sleeping on, and stop against the wall directly under the hanging keys.

Perry punched the air as if he had just scored the winning penalty in a final. He imagined the applause and cries from thousands of supporters who were now chanting his name. But that was the easy part, now it was time for phase two, which Perry was far from confident about.

He picked up the vintage fishing rod, which was shaking slightly, such was his nervousness. As hoped, the rod was long enough as he pointed it towards his target, always keeping it above the sleeping head of Grubbins. From the pole dangled the fishing line and hook that he would attempt to snare the keyring with. He came close, again and again but just failed, beads of sweat now appeared on Perrys forehead; how long did he have before Grubbins snapped awake. After another few close, but frustrating failures, he finally managed to latch it on.

He pulled the fishing rod up once, twice, three times before he managed to lift the keys off the peg. He had wanted to merely dislodge them, for them to fall into the hat sitting below, but now they were stuck on the fishing hook. This was a terrible plan he admitted to himself. There was only one thing for it, he would just have to pull the fishing rod and keys out of the room. However, Perry soon realised this was not going to be possible.

If the hotel had a lock, then Grubbins had the key. You could usually hear him coming minutes before he appeared. The sheer weight of the keyring was enormous. Far heavier than any thrashing fish this old rod had ever attempted to catch. What little strength Perry had was running out, the fishing rod itself was bending under the tremendous pressure. There was just no way he was going to be able to lift it over the sleeping head of Grubbins. He was at an impasse.

'Please, please, please... don't get it stuck in Grubbins sideburn hedge...'

Sweat was trickling down the back of Perry's neck, his face red, his arms burning. Any second he was going to smack Grubbins across the head and wake him up and then it was game over. There was a sudden twang....

Whop-eesh

... and the fishing rod almost leapt out of his hands. The old line had finally snapped under the weight and thankfully for Perry the keys had fallen, with barely a jangle, into the hat waiting for them below.

Perry couldn't believe he had any luck left. He carefully guided the fishing rod out of the room and laid it at his feet. Now to retrieve the keys nestling within the hat. This he had already prepared for. Prior to sliding the hat into the room, Perry had tied a loop of string around it and now all he had to do was carefully pull the hat out.

The hat and roller skate combination had done its job and it wheeled itself out without incident. More importantly, Grubbins had never even batted an eyelid. If anything, his snoring had helped him mask the theft.

Perry quickly identified the key he was after; it being slightly rusted and much larger than any of the others. It wasn't easy but he finally managed to remove it from the keyring and place it safely in his pocket. This was now the weakest part of his plan, or so he had previously thought. He certainly couldn't risk putting the keys back on the wall so instead he placed them gently on the floor by the door. When Grubbins woke up and looked for his keys he would eventually spot them lying there. Hopefully he would just scratch his head and think they had fallen off his belt, forgetting he had hung them up.

Mission accomplished; an elated Perry snuck down the hall with the tools of his trade. When he was out of earshot, he slipped his shoes back on.

SQUEAK...
SQUEAL...
CHEEP...

SQUEAK...
SQUEAL...
CHEEP...

As expected, they started to shout and wail in protest. Perry suddenly understood something for the first time. So that's why he's called the Plimsoll Bandit...

What a sheer piece of audacity. That plan should never have worked. I am writing this and even I cannot quite believe it. I have no idea how you are getting on. HB

Chapter 20

No power had yet been restored to the hotel, and with the weather getting progressively worse, it was safe to assume they were going to have to get used to the situation for the rest of the night. Perry, still exhilarated from his earlier success, couldn't focus on anything more than reading comics by candlelight in his room. Even when he found that too taxing, he instead fantasised about running the hotel with his mum and dad. The rusting lump of metal that he had hidden under his pillow, being the literal key to his future happiness.

Soon enough, it was almost time for Perry to begin working again. He arranged another unsuccessful attempt to tame his wild hair and gave his new uniform a thorough check. He needed to ensure there was nothing amiss that would give Uncle Hugo an excuse to berate him, not that he generally needed one. All set, he gave himself a wink in the mirror and then headed downstairs.

He timed it perfectly, taking up his spot in the corner of the drawing room just as Jimmy James Jr. and Ms Harrumph arrived.

Meanwhile, an under the weather Sorry Noakes, stumbled down the stairs into reception. He couldn't believe it was dinner time already and wasn't sure he was up to the challenge. He clutched his bloated tummy, which was fighting against the constraints of his buttons and belt.

'Are you okay sir?' asked Erstwhile, who stood behind the reception desk. He had seen enough of Belinda's handywork to spot the telltale green pallor on Mr Noakes face. A look, when combined with the brown suit, resulted in a quaint camouflage effect.

A piercing pain dug into Sorry's intestines and spread out to both sides. He doubled over in agony, completely winded. He looked towards Erstwhile for help, eyes tearing with the discomfort.

'The toilets are just down there,' pointed Erstwhile to the corridor next to the stairs. Sorry took off in a green and brown blur.

Sorry Noakes cursed the name of one Hugo BUMbler, as he barged into the toilet cubicle. Sitting there, beads of sweat peppering his face, he cursed him again for good measure. At one point, as he waited for his terrible ordeal to end, he was forced to use his tie to cover his nose and mouth. If he never saw that BUMblers stupid sprout loving face again, it would be too soon. Only then did he notice the huge painting of Hugo affixed to the wall, staring down at him, grinning inanely.

In the drawing room, Jimmy James Jr. was trying his best to engage Ms Harrumph in conversation, his hands gesticulating wildly, no doubt on the serenity one could achieve from eating with a spork. They stood at the bar where, as usual, Grubbins could be found vigorously polishing a wine glass with a rag of dubious cleanliness. Perry wondered if said slender wine glass had once started off the journey as a rugged pint glass, Grubbins did enjoy a powerful polish.

'I GUESS I SHOULD BE THANKFUL ALL THAT BOTTOM FLASHING EARLIER CRUSHED MY APPETITE. I DON'T FEEL TOO ILL.

Grubbins served her a drink as her eyes seemed to scan the room, looking to be anywhere but here.

To relieve the boredom, Perry had retreated into his own little world. He now found himself asking if there had been another round of thunder.

It had been his Uncle Hugo ringing the dinner gong which caused the distracted Perry to jump.

KA-BOOOOO

NNNNGGG

Uncle Hugo was an eccentric, or perhaps the truth was that he liked to play the part of one. He stood there, golden gong in hand, adorned in a purple velvet tuxedo for the evening. His hair was slicked and parted to each side, his moustache was still sub par and the buttons on his overly tight jacket looked like they were going to shoot off for freedom at any moment. Amusement aside, this had the potential for a real health and safety issue.

'Welcome everyone,' greeted Uncle Hugo to his captive audience, 'I'm glad you could all make it. I hope you managed to get some rest under the circumstances,' and as if to make the point his nemesis - the patio doors - rattled again.

'As you can hear, the storm has not abated and alas there has been no word on the power situation, but I'm sure the relevant people are all hard at work on it.'

'Can't... Can't you get a phone signal in this place,' complained a weary looking Sorry Noakes, as he skuttled crab like into the room. 'I've been trying since I arrived here, not even a single bar.'

'I'm sorry,' said Uncle Hugo.

Perry closed his eyes and waited...

'No... No,' replied Sorry, as if offended, 'I'M Sorry.'

'Of course you are,' said Uncle Hugo, not prepared to go around in that circle again. 'What I mean is that this hotel, as the name suggests, and as you have experienced, is rather remote. A beautiful location to be sure, but phone signals or internet coverage is not for us. It's a complete dead zone, always has been. But I much prefer it that way, sharpens the mind I feel.'

Oh, how many times had Perry heard that speech. He was the only kid at school who didn't have internet, he may as well have been a caveman. Another reason why he loved popping down into the village to visit Malaika, the Wi-Fi!

'What... What a nuisance,' grumbled Sorry, 'I have things to organise for the convention you know.'

'I'm sure you do,' said Uncle Hugo fawning, but not caring. 'I'm sure this storm will blow itself out overnight and in the morning the weather will be idyllic. You'll be able to get a signal in the village or perhaps, if truly desperate, you can of course use our landline, for only a small charge,' he added.

'Now everyone,' he said clapping his hands as if addressing a group of children, 'are we all here? Our Belinda has prepared for us another excellent repast, considering the conditions, in fact I can smell the roast chicken from here.' He rubbed his belly with vigour. Perry moved slightly to the right, out of the line of fire, just in case one of the buttons made an explosive break for it.

'Mr Gentle-Me isn't here,' pointed out Grubbins, using up his quota of spoken words for the week. He was now attempting to polish another glass into non-existence.

'LUCKY HIM,' said Ms Harrumph sarcastically.

'It's good life decisions like that which has allowed him to grow up to be a fossil,' agreed Jimmy James Jr.

I... I wish I could join him,' grumbled Sorry Noakes, who was holding his stomach again.

Uncle Hugo snapped his fingers professionally. Meaning it was loud, sharp, clear, filled with purpose, the right amount of authority and with years of practice. It was a snap of the fingers that was to be obeyed. Perry walked over to his uncle who grabbed him by the shoulders and whispered in his ear.

'Get up to Mr Gentle-Me's room. That old fool has obviously slept in. Remind him we are dining presently; we will not wait.'

With that he gave Perry a shove towards reception.

'Everyone, if you wouldn't mind making your way over to the dining room.'

On cue, the three guests all shuffled off towards their fate, leaving Uncle Hugo in their wake.

'Grubbins! Those majestic, mutated, mutton chops of yours need a pair of garden shears to them. You'll soon not be able to fit through the door frame. You look like you have stapled a sheep to each cheek.'

'Thank you M'lud,' he smiled.

Perry, meanwhile, was climbing the stairs from reception one by one.

SQUEAK... **SQUEAL...** CHEEP...

Mr Gentle-Me's room was on the 2nd floor. When he finally reached it, he gave it a soft knock. There was no reply. He tried again, slightly harder, imagining each knock as one of his uncle's annoying finger snaps. Still nothing.

'Hello Mr Gentle-Me,' said Perry, his face pressed up against the door. 'I've just come to remind you that it's dinner time. Will you be joining us?'

As he waited for some form of reply, Perry looked up and down the corridor, the candle he held was causing shadows to flicker along the walls, as if they were creeping towards him. He was about to try another knock when he remembered what his uncle had said about him sleeping in. Perry tried the handle and found it unlocked.

It opened quietly and he pushed on into the room. A room in complete darkness, Mr Gentle-Me's own candle must have gone out. Perry held his one high as he waved it back and forth.

'Mr Gentle-Me,' there was no response, but he did see a lump in the bed. His uncle was right, the old salesman had fallen asleep. But what should he do? Would it be bad manners to wake him up? He didn't want to give him a fright. Still, he couldn't let him miss dinner either. He had observed him during lunch, and he had eaten nothing, he must be hungry now, surely. His uncle's words fluttered back into his head - *we will not wait* - Perry decided he would not give his uncle the satisfaction.

Perry moved slowly over to the bed, not wanting to trip over anything in the gloom. He would give him a little shake on the shoulder and announce himself. Perry did just that. Nothing. He tried again.

'Mr Gentle-Me, sorry to wake you,' (firm shake). 'It's time for dinner Mr Gentle-Me.' (hard shake). Nothing.

Perry was impressed, he knew he could be hard to rouse for school, but this was on another level. He decided to walk round to the other side of the bed where Mr Gentle-Me was facing, perhaps the light from the candle would help wake him. If not, then his annoying shoes would.

SQUEAK... **SQUEAL...** **CHEEP**...

SQUEAK... **SQUEAL...** **CHEEP**...

There was still no response. Mr Gentle-Me looked to have changed into pyjamas and his wig had been carefully placed atop the bedside cabinet. It all seemed very orderly but then Perry froze. Mr Gentle-Me was very pale. He looked asleep but Perry couldn't see or hear him breathing. Then he noticed them, red marks on Mr Gentle-Me's throat. He must have choked in his sleep. Perry summoned up the nerve and quickly poked him in the forehead. Nothing.

Perry flew out of the room as if the ghost of Mr Gentle-Me had risen from his slumber and screamed in his face. His speed was so fast, his candle was snuffed out in an instant and his shoes didn't have the opportunity to give their usual protest. The encroaching shade only spurred him on as he threw himself dangerously down the stairs as fast as he ever had and didn't stop until he burst into the dining room, never so glad as to be in the company of people again. Well, at least moving ones.

'What on Earth boy,' roared Uncle Hugo, furious at this breach in etiquette.

Perry was bent over, out of breath, trembling and panting. Uncle Hugo was incandescent at his behaviour and continued to stare daggers at him. Perry's father, however, instantly knew something was amiss.

'Perry, what's happened?' he asked calmly.

'It's... it's Mr Gentle-Me,' he stammered. Perry was still struggling for breath.

'It's okay son, slow down, everything is okay, just tell us what's happened.'

'It's... it's Mr Gentle-Me. I went to wake Mr Gentle-Me, but he wouldn't. He wouldn't wake up. He's DEAD!'

Well I never, as in I never saw that coming. Did you? This is truly gripping, even if I do say so myself. And I just did, which makes it fact. HB

Chapter 21

Malaika tried her very best, but under these conditions it was almost one sluggish step forward and two quickly forced steps backward. At this rate, thanks to this fierce deluge, she almost expected to end up back at her house rather than up at the hotel.

Despite the hour it was as dark as night; the trees were bent almost double with the ferocity of the wind. A driving torrent of rain forced her head down as she slowly trudged forward. Again and again, she had to remind herself exactly why she was out here.

On a day like this she would have liked nothing better than to be lying on her bed, warm and dry, reading a scary book. The bombshell that her mother had texted her had changed everything. This was big news. A game changer. It was as dangerous as this storm and Perry, along with everyone else at the hotel, needed to be made aware.

Leaves were shooting and whizzing past her like daggers. She hugged herself tightly and continued to fight against the elements. She had to pull up the hood of her yellow raincoat again to offer her some protection. She hated to think what had already impaled itself in her hair.

Slowly but surely, above the sound of the howling wind and the lashing rain, she began to hear a terrible roaring. It wasn't until she got to the bridge that she understood why. The river had in parts burst its banks, it had swelled and was running faster than she had ever seen it before.

The dirty looking churning water was mesmerising to watch, she couldn't take her eyes off it. Something made her though. A swaying motion, subtle, but movement none the less. Malaika thought it was just the wind but then she saw it with her own eyes. It was the bridge itself.

The horrific weather, the terrifying wind, the sheer rapid force of the river, it was taking its toll. The bridge looked like it was starting to breakdown and collapse. Malaika gave up her fight against the gale and allowed it to help her back away, off the bridge and on to, if not dry land, certainly solid land.

There was no way she could try and cross that, it was far too dangerous. She desperately wanted to get to the hotel, she wanted to warn Perry, but things were starting to get out of hand. She would have to leave it to the police to deal with, it was what she should have done in the first place.

She turned away from the crumbling bridge, allowing the rain to beat on her back. Despite the protection she wore it was still insufficient for a day like this and she was drenched. Her wellington boots were filling up with water and every step she took made her feet slosh about inside them. Malaika began to take a few of those sloshing steps forward towards home, when she thought she heard a whimpering noise. No, it was the hurricane like winds playing tricks on her and she continued on her way. But then she heard something again, this time it was a bark. Malaika forced herself to turn around and a timely flash of lightning across the cloudy sky allowed her to see it through clenched eyes.

There, sitting in the middle of the creaking bridge was Pretzel. The silly dog must have followed her up from the village. He normally looked like he had been dragged through a hedge backwards, short wiry hair sticking out and facing every point on a compass at once, she almost didn't recognise him. Now, he was shivering, soaked to the bone, and scared out of his wits.

'Pretzel, come here.'

'Pretzel, here boy.'

Malaika shouted at him, screamed at him, even pulled out a now soggy dog treat she found in her pocket. But he didn't move. He was rooted to the spot. He either couldn't hear her over the roar of the river, or most likely was too terrified to move in either direction.

At that precise moment a large chunk of stone masonry toppled from the side of the bridge and disappeared into the frothy murky depths below. Malaika bit her knuckle. This old thing didn't have long left, it was going to collapse. Pretzel's frightened bark sealed it, she had to save him.

She understood that adding her weight to the disintegrating bridge could well be the straw that broke the camels back, but she had no choice, she had to rescue Pretzel. She took a tentative step back on to the rickety structure, then another and slowly another. A further section of the bridge fell away into the roiling darkness. Malaika took a leaf out of Pretzels book and stood there herself, rooted to the spot, transfixed, uncertain, her heart about to burst out of her chest.

'**Do you hear me feet,**' she shouted. They refused to move. '**It's now or never.**'

The bridge began to violently sway. It was tearing itself apart from the other side of the bank. Mother nature was easily winning this battle.

Surprising even herself, she soon realised she was moving, running, sprinting, as fast as the conditions and her heavy water filled boots allowed. Onwards into the biting rain which was making everything seem like it was moving in slow motion. Her legs were pumping, she was building up speed and momentum. She swooped up a startled Pretzel with one hand and continued. She was almost across.

Suddenly the whole bridge began to implode and fall into the water. She was at the end of the line. No more bridge. She leapt into the void...

That was a dashing, brave deed. I must admit, I would have stood to the side and saluted the little dog as it began its long journey out to sea. It would have been an old sea dog – ooh arrr. HB

Chapter 22

Perry looked at his father, then turned to the frozen guests. They had been busy poking at a starter of mystery pâté on burnt toast. Except for Jimmy James Jr. who currently had an enormous slice of unripe melon wedged in his mouth. He looked like a grinning clown.

They all stared back at Perry as if he was making some form of joke and were now awaiting the punchline.

'Mr Gentle-Me is dead,' repeated Perry.

'**Eeeek...,**' went Sorry Noakes, who shrank into his chair, causing a piece of grey slimy pâté to drip from his wiry moustache.

'Erstwhile,' snarled Uncle Hugo, his face like thunder, 'deal with this.'

Everyone moved on mass, much to Uncle Hugo's annoyance and before you knew it, there was a slow candle lit pilgrimage marching upstairs following Perry's father.

'I'M NOT SURE WE SHOULD BE GATHERED TOGETHER SO CLOSELY. ESPECIALLY AMONGST THESE NAKED FLAMES. IT COULD BE DISASTEROUS,' Ms Harrumph cautioned.

'As adults, I'm sure everyone can hold it in until they are in the privacy of their own rooms,' said a naive Jimmy James Jr.

A voice from behind shouted 'Hey... Hey, can you all hurry up... I'm not feeling too good.'

Perry's dad finally stopped at the entrance to Mr Gentle-Me's door and gave it a loud knock. There was no answer.

'Well,' said Uncle Hugo impatiently from the end of the queue. 'If he's dead he's not going to open the door for you, go in and check.'

Perry watched his dad walk into the room.

'Mr Gentle-Me, can you hear me?'

Silence.

He strode over to the bed and looked at the still figure of Mr Gentle-Me. Everyone else was now shuffling into the room trying to get a better look.

'OOOF! THIS RATE OF DECOMPOSITION IS NOT POSSIBLE. WE ONLY SAW HIM A FEW HOURS AGO. THIS BODY SMELLS LIKE IT HAS BEEN ROTTING FOR WEEKS...'

'I'm... I'm afraid that that was me,' offered Sorry Noakes sheepishly. He drew dirty looks from everyone.

'Please, have a little respect,' said Perry's father.

'Was it old age, I bet it was old age, back home people die of old age all the time.'

'A... A hit and run?'

'THE COOKING?'

'Maybe it was a lightning bolt, you know, with the weather outside.'

'A... A shark attack?'

'THE COOKING I TELL YOU.'

Everyone started throwing around wild theories as to the demise of Mr Gentle-Me.

'How about murder,' replied Perry's father, which managed to shut everyone up.

'What are you talking about,' said Uncle Hugo who was twiddling with his bow tie.

'Look at this, his throat, see those marks, red and starting to bruise. I think Mr Gentle-Me may have been strangled.'

'WHAAAT! STRANGLED! HE MAY HAVE BEEN SIMPLY CLAWING AT HIS OWN THROAT. I KNOW I WAS EARLIER. MY SENSE OF TASTE HAS STILL NOT RETURNED.'

'Gee whiz, a murder! This is just like something from a TV show' said an excited Jimmy James Jr.

'Calm down everyone,' cried Uncle Hugo. 'Let's not start jumping to conclusions here. The High Hill Hotel has a strict no murder policy. Well, ever since the serial killer Futon Bumbler was apprehended.'

There was another flash, followed by the rumble of thunder.

'**Eeeek...,**' cried Sorry Noakes who went weak at the knees and was caught by Jimmy James Jr.

'VERY WELL, PERHAPS A KILLER DOES LINGER WITHIN OUR MIDST,' Ms Harrumph stated matter-of-factly.

Suspicious glances were shared and traded around the room as a fog of distrust fell among them. The flickering candlelight casting a grotesque pallor across their faces.

'Enough of this, enough,' said Uncle Hugo. 'We will all, calmly, walk downstairs. We will phone the authorities and leave Mr Gentle-Me here in peace. We will cease jumping to conclusions. Don't deny it, I heard one of you cast aspersions on the cooking! When the police arrive, they can investigate and decide if anything suspicious is at play here. Until then there will be no more talk of murder. That could just be a rash on his neck.'

From what he had seen earlier, even Perry knew that was a weak excuse.

Uncle Hugo turned, walked out of the room and snapped his fingers. 'Come everyone, out, out.'

'Yes, this could well be a crime scene, best to leave and not contaminate it any further,' said Perry's dad, not exactly giving in to his brother.

Everyone mobilised out of the room, no one wanting to be the last one left with the body. They all trooped back downstairs and gathered in reception. Perry's father addressed them all.

'I'll give the police a call now, I suggest everyone retire to the drawing room, make yourself comfortable and await their arrival.' Everyone nodded in silent agreement.

'Yes, poor Mr Gentle-Me,' piped in Uncle Hugo, 'Desiccated by life, but at the end so full of vigour. I suggest you make the call brother, and we all go and finish dinner. I'm famished, I

don't know about you lot. I'm also sure this is what he would have wanted.'

How typical of his uncle thought Perry to himself.

His dad went to the reception desk, picked up the phone and dialled the number for the village police station. Outside, the driving wind and rain continued unabated. Everyone continued to stand in total silence. It was obvious from his incessant fidgeting that Uncle Hugo was bursting to start eating again.

'Hello,' said his father. 'Hello, can you hear me? Hello... listen, it's Erstwhile Bumbler calling from the High Hill Hotel... hello.'

CRAAAACCKKLEEE.... went the line.

'Hello,' he persisted. 'It's the High Hill Hotel here, is this the police station?'

CRAAAAACCKKLEEE...

'We have a dead body here. I repeat, we have a dead body. We need help. Possible murder. Can you hear me, is there anyone there...'

CRAAAACCKKLEEE...

'Hello, we need help, we need...'

CRAAAACCKKLEEE... BEEP... BEEP... BEEP... BEEP...CLICK.

Everyone could hear the line go dead.

'Oh... Oh no,' whispered Sorry Noakes.

'What's happened?' said Uncle Hugo. He stood there munching on a piece of toast he had enchanted from somewhere.

'The phone is dead,' said Perry's father, carefully replacing the handset. He instantly picked it up again, but there was nothing. No ringtone. It was disconnected. 'The landline is down.'

'Did they hear you?' asked Jimmy James Jr. who was stroking his beard in concern.

'I honestly don't know, I'm sure they picked it up, I tried but I can't tell, no one was speaking back to me, then the phone just cut off. Must have been the weather, first the power and now the phone.'

'WHAAAT! YOU HOPE IT WAS THE WEATHER YOU MEAN,' blared Ms Harrumph.

'What do you mean?' spluttered Uncle Hugo through a mouthful of crumbs, spraying them in the direction of everyone near him. 'Of course it was the weather, it's as plain to see as your expansive forehead.'

'WHAAAT! IT COULD BE THE MURDERER OF COURSE. HIS CRIME NOW DISCOVERED; HE HAS CUT OFF THE TELEPHONE LINE TO ENSURE WE CANNOT CONTACT THE AUTHORITIES. NOT UNTIL HE HAS FINISHED WITH ALL OF US.'

'**Eeeek...**' squeaked Sorry Noakes, going weak at the knees yet again. Thankfully Jimmy James Jr. was on hand to catch him for the second time.

'There is only one option now,' said Perry's dad who reappeared with a jacket. 'I'll have to go down to the village myself and bring them back.'

'No Dad,' begged Perry.

'I have to, the weather outside is nothing compared to what is going on inside this hotel.'

'WHAAAT! THE KILLER COULD BE OUTSIDE WAITING FOR YOU,' blasted Ms Harrumph.

'You really need to get out of this negative thinking cycle,' offered Jimmy James Jr.

The room was getting quite worked up now, including Perry who was concerned for his father's safety. Then, the unexpected happened.

doom...

doom...

doom...

There was a banging on the hotel door...

I would like to take this opportunity to apologise. I always try to avoid 'toilet humour'. I find it a meagre and unsophisticated way of injecting infantile jokes into the narrative. However, the story goes where the story takes us. Plus, as it is loosely based on the truth, my hands were slightly tied. So, hold your breath and strap yourselves in. HB

Chapter 23

There was a spontaneous round of applause in reception.

'They... They did hear you,' grinned Sorry Noakes, delighted that he was going to be saved.

'Gee whiz, police that knock, that's so quaint, said Jimmy James Jr. 'Excellent service though, I guess with your country being so small it doesn't take them long, it's only been a few minutes.'

'WHAAAT!' erupted Ms Harrumph, 'IT CAN'T POSSIBLY BE THE POLICE YET. MORE LIKELY IT IS THE KILLER, TRYING TO GET BACK INSIDE, NOW THAT WE HAVE BEEN FORCED TO SECURE THE BUILDING.'

The round of applause was now a dim and distant memory.

Perry watched as his father was the first to move, he slowly approached the door and reached out for the key.

Everyone suddenly burst into action. Sorry Noakes struggled, but managed, to pick up a chair as a potential shield. Uncle Hugo grabbed the nearest thing to him which was a vase. Jimmy James Jr. selected an umbrella from the stand as a makeshift sword. Ms Harrumph plunged her hand into her bag and began rummaging around. Finally, she pulled out what appeared to be a handful of stones.

'You... You carry rocks in your handbag?'

'NO, NOT ROCKS. THIS IS IGNEOUS FUDGE. NOT TO BE CHEWED - SUCKED ONLY.'

'Are... Are you going to throw it and hope he eats it?'

'NO, YOU HAVE SURELY HEARD THE TALE OF DAVID AND GOLIATH. AND BEFORE YOU SAY ANYTHING, I AM DAVID IN THIS LITTLE SCENARIO.'

The door key was slowly turned and then the locks at the top and bottom of the entrance were unlatched. Perry's father then pulled the thick heavy-set door open with all his strength. He was rewarded with a torrent of rain and wind.

'Quickly, close it,' begged Uncle Hugo, obviously having a flashback to earlier in the day.

Perry's dad reached out into the darkness and grabbed the figure who was standing outside and pulled them in as he began wrestling with the door to get it closed again.

Said figure was small and had excessive rainwater dripping off their yellow slicker.

'Identify yourself,' demanded Uncle Hugo who raised his vase as if to throw it.

'It's me,' came a quiet shivering voice.

'Malaika,' cried Perry, who ran towards her.

'The one and only,' she replied. She placed what she was carrying on to the ground and let the coat drop off her to the floor, it lay there in a growing puddle of water.

Perry gave her wide smile and a big hug, despite the wetness she smelled of cherry bubble-gum and hope. 'Don't be offended but you look like a drowned rat.'

'No... No,' squealed Sorry Noakes pointing, 'over there, that's a drowned rat, filthy, filthy vermin.' He performed a timorous dance behind the chair as he held it out to protect him from the beast.

'No,' replied Malaika, 'that's Pretzel, he's very much a dog and it would be appreciated if someone could get him a towel before he...'

She didn't get to complete her sentence as Pretzel gave himself an almighty shake. An unbelievable deluge of rainwater was showered across the room, most of it going over Uncle Hugo who he had snuck up next to.

'What... what... what,' was all a shocked Uncle Hugo could muster at the sudden downpour.

'Boy, it's terrible outside, really terrible. Why was the door locked though?' she grumbled.

'To stop the wind from blowing it open,' explained Perry.

'Everything was being blown wide open mam,' said Jimmy James Jr. as he looked at Uncle Hugo.

'And what's with all the candles, is there something wrong with your lights?'

'We had a power cut up here, we assumed it would be the same down in the village as well, obviously not. But what are you doing here?' asked Perry.

'Oh, that's charming,' she said.

'Sorry, I didn't mean it like that, what made you come up here in such terrible weather, it must have been dangerous.'

'It was, believe me.'

'Well, I'm afraid to say mam, it might be even more dangerous here,' said Jimmy James Jr.

Grubbins misunderstood the remark and nodded solemnly, he could feel the foul unpleasant smog which was slowly starting to build and take hold. Belinda had really done it this time.

Malaika didn't understand the warning either, so continued with her story.

'I just had to come here Perry. There has been a... development.'

'A development,' chimed in Uncle Hugo who had finished brushing as much of the water from his tuxedo as he could.

'WHAAAT! DOES IT INVOLVE THE POLICE BY ANY CHANCE? ARE THEY ON THEIR WAY HERE?'

'Well,' said Malaika, still unsure as to the line of questioning, 'it does in a way.'

'Before you tell us, there is something we need to tell you,' admitted Perry's father. He had picked up Malaika's discarded coat and Grubbins was already mopping up the puddle of water on the floor. He was also glaring at the dog as if he recognised it.

There came a large and loud sneeze from somewhere in the room.

'I'm... I'm allergic to dogs,' said Sorry, who sneezed again as if trying to prove a point. He pulled a sock from his pocket and blew his nose. An annoying raspy noise that grated in the ears.

'Are you using a sock to blow your nose?' remarked Uncle Hugo in astonishment.

'Well... Well, it's not a pair of underpants is it. Of course it is not a sock. This is my own invention. It's a sockerchief, and when it gets a bit full, you can just turn it inside out.'

'I'm not sure whether to buy one or clip you round the ear,' ushered Uncle Hugo, who didn't know what to make of Sorry's remark.

'Between... Between you and I, it's a sale I'm hoping for.'

Perry's father tried his best to blot out the nonsense around him.

'As I was saying, one of our guests has unfortunately passed away,' he continued. 'It may or may not have been natural.'

'Not... natural?' queried Malaika, eyes wide.

'He means murdered,' clarified Perry, 'Mr Gentle-Me, I found him earlier, in his bed. Strangled.'

'Strangled!' shouted Malaika.

'Yes, sorry to spook you,' said Perry's dad, 'but my son is correct, well, potentially strangled. I was trying to phone the police, but the line went dead, and we were cut off. I'm just about to head down to the village to bring them.'

'Oh,' said Malaika putting her hand to her mouth, 'you can't, you can't go.'

'I'm sorry?' he replied and instantly pointed his finger at Sorry Noakes, as if daring him to say anything.

'You can't go Mr Bumbler, it's not possible, it's the bridge, it's gone, washed away.'

'Gone!' said Uncle Hugo in disbelief.

'I saw it myself. I was on it. I managed to jump clear just in time and make it to the other side.'

'Does this mean what I think it means,' asked Jimmy James Jr.

'Yes,' said Uncle Hugo, 'if this girl is to be taken at her word, then it means we are all stranded here.'

'This... This is not good,' whimpered Sorry Noakes who was beginning to sweat profusely.

'Don't worry my friend, stay positive, there is a natural balance to everything. Something good will happen soon. Just focus on your mental lucidity.' Jimmy James Jr. put his arm around the much smaller Sorry Noakes, who inwardly shuddered at the cascade of long blonde hair that fell over him.

'I'm glad you are okay, that was very brave of you, but what made you risk everything to come up here?' asked Perry.

'Well, my mum texted me from the police station, she was over there cleaning, and she knows all about my little... hobby,' she winked at Perry.

'Are you referring to the stolen treasure that may be hidden here,' growled Uncle Hugo. 'I'm not stupid you know, I'm aware you were wandering the grounds last year with that ridiculous contraption. Although if memory serves you did find some spoons, so it wasn't a total waste of your time.'

'Well, you can believe it or not,' Malaika snapped back, 'the fact of the matter is many people do believe it and one of them is coming here.'

'And who would that be?' asked Uncle Hugo smugly.

'Only the ex-cell mate of the person who stole it. He somehow got out on good behaviour. The police were secretly following him, hoping he might lead them to it, and he was last seen heading in the direction of Little Didwob.'

'WHAAAT!' barked Ms Harrumph.

'And is he here?' asked Perry's father.

'They are not sure,' sighed Malaika, 'it was earlier this morning, but then their computers all went down, nothing to do with the weather, it was a computer virus I think.'

'Unbelievable,' said Uncle Hugo looking more and more exasperated. 'A bunch of nitwits, the whole lot of them.'

'So... So,' began Sorry Noakes nervously, 'this person could be here by now?'

'Very unlikely,' cut in Uncle Hugo, 'I'm sure he is nowhere near the village, never mind this hotel.'

'I'm not so sure, in fact I do very much believe he is here,' said Malaika.

'And why is that?' snapped Uncle Hugo.

'Because the name of the cell mate was Billy Nettle, she replied.'

There was silence in the room.

'WHAAAT! THE TV WEATHERMAN?'

'No...No, that wasn't his name. It's the one from the garden show. Always flashing his bottom cleavage when he's picking up weeds. Very distasteful, but what do you expect from that channel,' said Sorry Noakes looking around for agreement.

Not to be outdone Jimmy James Jr. added 'Back home I had a next-door neighbour who had a brother called Billy, I doubt it would be him though. He fits tyres.'

'SSSSSHHH...' commanded Ms Harrumph.

'I've heard of him Miss,' said Grubbins, his usually weathered ruddy face now looked grey.

'Well, do tell,' mocked Uncle Hugo.

Malaika motioned for him to continue.

Billy Nettle, a killer, but that's not what the press called him, oh they had a far catchier name for him,' and he looked back towards Malaika.

'The Sopwith Strangler,' she announced.

The Sopwith Strangler, now that is a troublesome blast from the past. Believe me, this book needs as much dramatic tension as possible, but still, how could they have released this man from his sentence early. Especially after everything he had done. Personally, I blame the politicians. If this psychotic ruffian is indeed within the confines of the hotel, then things are looking very grim for our unfortunate protagonists. HB

Chapter 24

Sorry Noakes fainted. He slumped to the floor as if his bones had turned to jelly. Not even Jimmy James Jr. was fast enough to catch him this time. Before anyone could do or say anything, Grubbins calmly walked over to the inert salesman and rubbed the wet mop he had been using in Sorry's face. After that he came to his senses rather quickly and embarrassingly stood back to his feet.

'Are you okay Mr Noakes, you seem to be a little... sweaty and shaky. Do have a sit down if this is all too much for you,' advised Uncle Hugo.

'Don't... Don't worry. My Psychiatrist, Dr Chernobyl, gave me some advise on coping mechanisms.'

'Mmm... okay, you just toddle off and sit over there on the reception stairs then,' Uncle Hugo dismissed him.

'THERE IS THE VERY STRONG POSSIBILITY THAT A MAD STRANGLER IS STALKING THIS HOTEL LOOKING FOR HIDDEN TREASURE AND DISPOSING OF ANYONE WHO GETS IN HIS WAY,' roared Philippa Harrumph.

'And he has already claimed his first victim,' gulped Jimmy James Jr.

'IT COULD BE FAR WORSE THAN THAT, DOES ANYONE KNOW WHAT THIS PERSON LOOKS LIKE. HE COULD EVEN BE ONE OF US!'

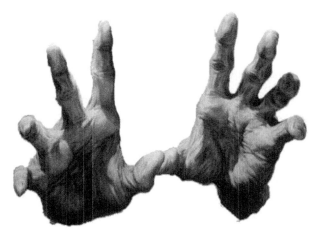

From the stairs Sorry Noakes looked intently at Jimmy James Jr.

In turn, Jimmy James Jr. stared suspiciously at Ms Harrumph.

Outraged at the very suggestion, Ms Harrumph pushed out her bosom.

Which caught the eye of Grubbins, who gazed captively.

Belinda, who had appeared from nowhere, furrowed her thick eyebrows and glared at Grubbins with her extra-large eye.

Round and round the wary stares continued, growing in intensity as faces strained and eyes bulged. It was very much in danger of developing into a gurning competition.

'ENOUGH,' cried Uncle Hugo. 'Everyone, please go into the drawing room. Girl, I'll have some towels delivered before you flood my hotel. I'll also have some sandwiches brought through, I'm not letting that chicken go to waste,' he murmured.

'WHAAAT! WHY BOTHER MAN. IF IT'S AS UNDERCOOKED AS THOSE SPROUTS EARLIER, IT WILL SOON WALK OUT AND JOIN US.'

Perry's dad came up to Malaika and whispered in her ear.

'Is that who I think it is?' he motioned towards Pretzel, who was vigorously sniffing the air around him.

Malaika nodded.

'I'm sorry Mr B, I was aware of the disgusting pong as soon as I was inside. Don't be too hard on him, he has been through a traumatic ordeal. But... oh... it's bad, isn't it. I'm really sorry.'

'I'll be honest with you Malaika, that wasn't him, you really have both come at a most unprecedented time. Okay, well before my brother realises who has joined us, I'll put him in my reception office and give him something to eat. He is still technically banned you know. I'm assuming he hasn't been toilet trained since his last appearance here?'

Malaika shook her head.

'Ah well, this night just keeps on getting better.' He then picked up the wet dog, keeping it at arms length to protect his suit. It began licking his hand, while he scratched it behind the ear, and they headed off towards his office.

Perry accompanied the sodden Malaika through to the drawing room.

'I can't believe this is happening, stuck in a hotel with a sadistic strangler,' said Perry.

'Yes, a sadistic strangler who's also looking for our treasure, which means our reward.'

'This has been a crazy, crazy day,' Perry shook his head.

Despite their recent bout of distrust, all three guests; Sorry Noakes, Jimmy James Jr. and Philippa Harrumph were now sitting in a group, their chairs all huddled together like encircled wagons searching for protection.

However, a disagreement was brewing. The combined weight of cabin fever and toxic sprout vapours were driving people to their limits.

'I CAN'T TAKE IT ANYMORE. ALL THOSE YEARS IN THE NAVY, EVEN IN SUBMARINES, IT WAS NOTHING LIKE THIS! I NEED AIR, FRESH AIR. OPEN THOSE PATIO DOORS.'

'No... No, there is a raging storm. Remember the last time. It's far too dangerous out there.'

'AND IT'S NOT IN HERE? PLEASE, LET US BREATHE. THIS IS CRUELTY.'

As promised, Perry's dad appeared with a bundle of fluffy towels.

'Here you go Malaika, get yourself dry. I'd say get yourself up to the fireplace but it's just for show, hasn't been used in years. I'll go upstairs and bring you down a spare pair of Perry's joggers and a t-shirt for you to change into.'

'Thanks Mr B, for one horrible moment I thought you were going to bring me down one of his spare uniforms' she said, covering herself in the towels.

'Ha-Ha, very funny. And Dad. Be careful!' Perry shouted after him.

Unobserved by anyone, Grubbins silently crept into the drawing room. He was carrying a tottering platter of untrustworthy looking sandwiches. Rammed tight into his pantaloon pockets were flasks of coffee and tea.

Uncle Hugo, stood silently at the fireplace chewing his fingernails. Then he caught sight of Grubbins. His eyes spasmed in disbelief.

'What is that over your face?' Uncle Hugo demanded to know.

'Mmmmfle mummmmple myddgle...'

'What are you saying? Get it off man, you look like a lunatic!'

Grubbins lifted the cloth above his mouth.

It's a gas mask M'lud. My own mother made this back when she used to work down at the old sprout factory. Dark days indeed. If you didn't wear something like this, with the foul corruptible reek, you could come down with the green nostril.'

Uncle Hugo just stared at him.

'The green nostril was nothing to be sniffed at, so to speak. After that was the path to madness. To think, these were originally a pair of my old Nans bloomers, can you believe it!'

'Finally, Grubbins. Finally, you have crossed the Rubicon. You are fired.'

'Oh, thank you M'lud, very kind of you.'

Perry and Malaika were also deep in conversation.

'I got the key,' Perry whispered.

'You what?'

'I have it, the key, for the catacombs. We will be able to get down there soon.'

'Seriously,' said Malaika. 'We have strangler on the prowl, and you want to go off into dark hidden parts of the hotel with this maniac on the loose?'

'We need to,' urged Perry. 'He knows where the museum exhibit is hidden. It's only a matter of time before he gets his hands on it. We need to find it Malaika, we need that reward money.'

'Perry, the chances of us finding it are already very slim. It's been successfully hidden for decades. Even if we did find it, he would just take it off our... dead bodies,' Malaika was beginning to hyperventilate.

'Beware the green nostril miss,' whispered Grubbins who had magically appeared beside them. 'Take this mask and save yourself.' He pressed it into her hand and then darted off to continue serving refreshments.

Perry could only shake his head. 'Listen, it will be okay, we can't give up, I won't give up. I want this hotel and I want my mum and dad to run it together.'

'I know,' said Malaika, 'and I'll help you in any way I can but isn't there a very good chance he may already have it.'

'What do you mean?'

'Well, why would the Sopwith Strangler do away with poor Mr Gentle-Me? In his room? In his bed? It must have been hidden in that room. He could have retrieved the treasure. He may even have left by now.'

'I don't want to think like that,' said Perry, although he knew she made a very good point. 'I was in the room though, it was dark, but it wasn't ransacked. I think it's still here and even if he does have it, perhaps he's not been able to get away, what with the bridge now gone.'

'I guess there is a chance,' admitted Malaika.

'Good, because even if I have to rugby tackle him to take it off him I will. The stakes are that high.'

There was another commotion from the corner of the drawing room where the guests had gathered. The sound of a chair being pushed over, was followed by an eerie cackling voice.

'Looky… Looky… Looky…'

Everyone turned in shock at this unannounced visitor. Only there wasn't anyone there, just Mr Noakes.

'I am a puppet… not a sock… My name… is Mr Frock… I cannot dance… I cannot walk… I have no mouth… but I can talk…'

Everyone was looking at Sorry Noakes, the shrill voice was coming from him, or was it? He wasn't alone. There, on his hand, was a sock puppet. It had a pair of black felt tip pen dots for eyes and around its midriff was a strip of pink taffeta, which crudely resembled a ballerina's tutu.

'WHAAAT IN THE 7TH LEVEL OF HELL IS THIS MONSTROSITY? QUICK, HE IS POSSESSED, DOES ANYONE HAVE HOLY WATER?' howled Ms Harrumph.

'Delighted to meet you all… I am Mr Frock… The Puppet Sock. … Looks like we are in a bit of a stink… Who is going to die next do you think…?

'What's with the creepy voice,' asked Jimmy James Jr.

'The voice? You only found the voice creepy?' challenged Malaika.

'Grubbins,' cried an ashen faced Uncle Hugo. 'Take Mr Noakes through to the dining room would you, until he has... calmed down.'

The usually unflappable Grubbins, threw up his eyebrows in alarm.

'Looky... Looky... Looky...'

Mr Frock was now staring at Grubbins belly button.

'You don't see many of those everyday...'

As a ventriloquist Sorry Noakes was terrible, but no one was laughing. If this was his coping mechanism, it was terrifying.

'Yes... M'lud,' replied Grubbins under duress. 'Would... you and... your friend like to come for a little walk?'

'Oh yes please... You look like a very nice man. Don't worry... We can shake off this Noakes loser. Are you single...?'

Nobody spoke whilst Grubbins escorted Mr Frock and the delicate Sorry Noakes from the drawing room. After they left, nobody still knew what to say.

I have seen many strange things in my time, but that, right there, was the weirdest thing I have seen since... last Tuesday. Sorry but I lead a fast paced and bizarre existence. I'm proud of it. HB

Chapter 25

An hour later, with some food and drink shared and no more terrifying surprises, everyone seemed a lot calmer. Perry's father decided this was the best time to address the room.

'Okay, so the situation seems to be as follows.

Outside we have a storm of almost biblical proportions.

Unfortunately, we could very well have a crazed strangler lurking inside.

We are cut off from the village.

The village is cut off from us.

We have no power.

We have no telephone.'

'We… We have no hope,' piped in Sorry Noakes, who was toying with his greasy locks. He had been allowed back into the fold, on the condition *Mr Frock* did not make a reappearance.

'There is always hope, but we need a plan of sorts. I appreciate it's no more than simply waiting it out until daylight and an end to this weather. But it's about how we do that. The way I see it, we have two options. We can all remain here tonight in the drawing room; it won't be comfy but safety in numbers and all that.'

'OR?' blasted Ms Harrumph.

'You can all retire to the safety of your rooms and remain there until morning.'

'I hate to be negative, it's not in my nature, but that didn't seem to work out too well for old Mr Gentle-Me,' said Jimmy James Jr. who was nibbling on a sandwich crust, the crumbs infused in his beard.

'Well, his door was not locked, there was no real need for it to be. This would be much different, you lock the door, even barricade yourself in if you want to. You don't need to open it for anyone and if someone was to try and get in, just shout and everyone will come running.'

The sheepish look on Sorry Noakes face revealed he wouldn't be running out of his room to help anyone anytime soon.

And so, the debate raged, back and forth until a consensus was reached. Everyone would go back to their room for the night. With everyone safely secured, Perry's dad and Grubbins would patrol the corridors of the hotel together until daylight.

With candles once again in hand, they all began the trip upstairs to their abode.

'Oh, not again,' complained Jimmy James Jr. who gagged on the fetid stench. 'Does no one have any self-control around here?'

'Oooh... Oooh I beg your forgiveness, Mr Self-Control Guru,' shouted Sorry Noakes. 'You have been eating this barbaric veggie nonsense for years, good for you if you are able to convert its vile evil side effects into 'positive vibes'. Everyday people, however, need to expel it. Flatulence is normal. There, I have said it. I am PROUD of it...'

With that he gave a rather ornate flourish of his hand and performed a deep graceful bow to his audience.

'NOOOOOOOO,' exploded Ms Harrumph.

This was not the only explosion, as Sorry Noakes birthed a bottom belch that reverberated throughout the stairwell. At least two of the candles spluttered, flared, and then leapt to twice their normal height, now purple in colour.

Perry watched in joy as each face along the line looked like it had just been slapped with a tramp's sweaty sock, or perhaps one of the 70 that Sorry Noakes was currently wearing.

The pace increased as they literally jogged, in stone silence, to their respectful floor. The first room reached was that of Jimmy James Jr. He motioned Sorry Noakes over to him.

'Right,' he whispered into his ear, 'no hard feelings, we are all in this together, now give it 30 minutes then come out of your room, I'll be standing outside waiting for you.'

'Are... Are you joking?'

'No, not at all. Look, they are just locking us up so we can't find this missing treasure. It's just sitting around here begging to be found. We'll be safe enough if we are together. Remember, 30 minutes.'

With that, he wished everyone a good night of peaceful sensory deprivation, ducked under the doorframe, closed his door, and turned his lock loudly.

'Mr Noakes,' said Perry's dad, 'I believe it's yourself next.'

'Yes... Yes, okay then.' He looked back down the corridor to the door of Jimmy James Jr., 'I'll see you all in the morning then, I guess.'

'One can but hope,' snarled Uncle Hugo as the door was closed and the lock turned.

'I'LL BE OKAY,' wailed Ms Harrumph as she strode onwards to her door. 'I PLAN TO DO A WORKOUT BEFORE RETIRING, I DO IT EVERYNIGHT, I TAKE MY EXERCISE VERY SERIOUSLY. AS IT'S STILL QUITE EARLY I MIGHT EVEN DO TWO SETS. I WOULD URGE YOU NOT TO DISTURB ME. I DO IT IN THE NUDE.' With that her door was slammed shut and the lock was turned.

Perry caught a departing smell of salty barnacles and driftwood.

It was then up to the 3rd floor, and they walked to Uncle Hugo's room first.

'Right, yes, well smashing, keep up the good work. Grubbins, I will call you if I need anything,' he said ignoring everyone else.

No sooner had he closed the door and turned the lock, when the sounds of furniture being moved rang out, no doubt directly behind the door.

Perry opened the door to his room, followed by Malaika and his dad.

'Okay,' he said to them both, 'that's everyone in their rooms, I don't expect them to come out until morning and the same applies to you. Grubbins and I will be close by so if you do need anything just shout. That door stays locked, and you do not open it for anyone but me, understand.'

'Only you,' repeated Perry, who gave his dad a hug. Perry made a big show of loudly locking the door behind him. He pressed his ear against it until he could hear his father and Grubbins wandering off.

'So now what?' asked Malaika, sitting on Perry's bed. 'Wow, this is one messy room, my mum would go bananas if I let it get into this state.'

'Well, my mum isn't here,' snapped Perry.

'I'm sorry,' said Malaika.

'No, ignore me,' replied Perry who stood next to her in the centre of the messy room. 'My nerves are getting the better of me.'

'So... we going to play a boardgame?'

'No time for that,' said Perry, '20 minutes I think and then we can sneak out, head downstairs and go down to the catacombs.'

'I can't believe we are going to do this. Have you never seen those scary films where they go into really dark dangerous places and you are sitting there going, look at those fools, they deserve what's going to happen to them?'

'Not really, I try not to watch those films.'

'Well, I'll spare you the details, but it doesn't end well for them.'

'Look, we will be fine. My dad is in earshot, there are two of us and we will be well equipped.'

'What do you mean?'

'I found these old working torches at the bottom of my toy chest,' he held them up. 'I also may have borrowed these from Uncle Hugo,' and there folded on his bed were a pair of high visibility vests and one hard hat, which he handed to Malaika.

'You weren't kidding,' she said.

'Oh, and we will need this,' Perry pulled the big key from underneath his pillow.

'This is starting to get exciting,' said Malaika.

'Well, I'm terrified,' said Perry. 'We go in 19 minutes...'

I firmly believe this young urchin is haunted by daft plans. Although I have to say it did remind me of that time when I had to improvise behind enemy lines. Suffice to say I saved the day and changed the course of the war. You will just have to take my word for it, the full report is heavily redacted. HB

Chapter 26

The creeping figure always kept to the shadows, which, thanks to the current blackout, did not pose much of a problem. Detection had been avoided on route through the hotel. They knew their luck might not last for long, however. Those who were either brave, or foolish enough, to be out of their rooms were blundering around like a herd of elephants. They had been easy enough to avoid, for now.

As expected, the kitchen was deserted, with the dishes from the abandoned dinner having been left unattended. A task for tomorrow no doubt if all survived the night.

The figure looked around, taking its time, ensuring no noise, the minimum of fuss and movement. This was not the moment to be discovered, there was still so much to be done.

Its purpose was resolute, and it glided over to the imposing looking stove. Dials and nobs were pulled, turned, and twisted until the sound of gas could be heard rustling into the room.

The dark figure then crept over to the other side of the kitchen where one of the extinguished candles sat. A lighter was quickly produced, and soon the candle was burning brightly.

One last look at the flickering candle and the hissing stove sent the silent figure confidently from the room, its job here was done. Now to find a suitable hiding place.

What tomfoolery is this? That is potentially very dangerous you know. Well, I am sorry, but I must make it very clear, for legal reasons, that I totally disavow myself from any and all actions carried out by these fictional characters, especially the ones acting totally irresponsibly. Now that I have that off my chest, I cannot wait to see what happens next, there will be fireworks, I am sure. HB

Chapter 27

The art of building a good barricade, believed Hugo, was to begin with a solid base. He frantically cast his eyes around the room, finally settling on the chest of drawers. He pulled, yanked, and dragged until it was positioned in front of the door. Then, on top of this, he carefully placed his bedside cabinet, a chair, a couple of pillows and a spare pair of pyjamas. By now he was a sweaty mess, but he still felt vulnerable. He then made the outrageous decision to try and haul the bed over, at which point something twanged in his back. He collapsed on to the mattress in pain, feeling sorry for himself, a small tear formed in his eye which...

...ran down Grubbins cheek as he laughed heartily. Despite the dire situation they found themselves in, Erstwhile couldn't help himself and smiled as well. A still chuckling Grubbins continued.

'And one other time, your brother said - Grubbins! Exactly what are those stains on your trousers? No, in fact, I don't want to know. I shudder to think what matter of depravity has been committed in those breaches - me too M'Lud, I replied. Ha-Ha-Ha. Your brother is a funny man Sir.' Grubbins dabbed at his wet face with his favourite cleaning rag.

'Well, that's one word to describe him,' replied Erstwhile trying to maintain some professionalism. They were slowly patrolling one of the many dark corridors of the hotel. 'A less generous assessment would say that his attitude...'

'... stinks, that foot is the very definition of gangrenous,' said Jimmy James Jr. who covered his mouth with his hand.

Sorry Noakes, had opened his door on time but was still not ready to go exploring, so ushered the fellow guest into his room. He explained he had suffered an itchy foot, which meant removing all his socks to scratch it. A time-consuming operation to say the least, he would not be ready to leave for another 20 minutes or so.

'I... I will admit it's a little off colour,' as he carefully put on the first sock from the large pile sitting before him.

'A little off colour! It's green!'

'I'm... I'm cursed. Yes, cursed with poor circulation.'

'Listen, you can't wear that many socks on your feet all day, it's not healthy. You are strangling them. You should be wearing sandals like I do. Having one's toes open to the environment is not only good for them, but it does wonders for your inner chakra. You won't catch me wearing socks and sandals.'

'You... You just haven't met the correct pair yet, let me tempt you...'

'No thank you. I am also a big believer in meditation over medication, but in your case it's too late for that, you better get yourself some professional help before they fall off.'

'And... And who exactly made you a doctor may I ask?'

'My nose, that's who, it's not only green but it has a shocking rancid smell!'

'I'll... I'll tell you what stinks, it's your...'

'PUMP...'

The noise was erupting from Ms Harrumphs room.

'PUMP IT UP, PUMP IT UP

1 - 2 - 3 - 4

NOW STRETCH...

PUSH IT, PUSH IT

ONE MORE TIME, GO ON, GO...'

'...on admit it,' said Malaika playfully as she punched Perry in the shoulder. They were heading down via the emergency back stairs to avoid running into Perry's father.

'I do not fancy you; I have no idea who in class said that but it's fake news.'

Malaika had found one way of avoiding the desperate horror of their situation and that was to wind up Perry, as much as she could, to take her mind off things.

'Oh, you so do Perry, everyone at school knows you fancy me. I see you sneaking looks at me all through the day.'

'I do not,' choked Perry, fighting to keep his volume under control. He could feel his face betraying him however, by his estimation it was approximately lobster red by now, hopefully in the gloom Malaika would fail to notice. He had no idea why she had brought this subject up on their way down from the room.

'You can always be honest with me Perry. Did you know that your face has gone all red?'

'It has not,' he lied, but he could feel it burning as if it had been slapped.

'That's so sweet, is it because you want to kiss me?'

'Malaika please, this is not the time and place, and my face is not red.'

'You are correct, it's now gone a bit purple, what does that mean?' Malaika had to hide her own face as a big smile broke out.

'It just means I'm a little out of breath, that's all. Right, that's us, we are almost here.' Finally, the stairs were at an end.

CLUNK-CLUNK

'Did you hear that?' gasped Malaika.

'No, I didn't. The heat radiating from my face must have deflected any sound.'

'WAIT! What's that?' cried Malaika. A shadow loomed before them. A figure standing there. 'It's the strangler, we need to run.'

A determined Perry instead raised his torch before him and gave a mighty sigh of relief.

'It's okay. It's just the suit of armour.'

'Why is it standing back here, in the middle of this hallway?' queried Malaika, her heart still racing.

'A good question. Obviously, someone's idea of a prank. Help me move it to the side so we can get passed.'

With a lot of grunting and a great deal of strain, they managed to shift the lump of rusty metal up against the wall.

'That thing weighs a ton,' complained Malaika.

'It surely does,' agreed Perry, who was panting for breath.

They now just had a small walk along this corridor, and they would be at the door leading to the catacombs. Perry fumbled with the key in his pocket, this was it, now or never.

Who has time for all this sneaking about? I appreciate a good story needs a little suspense, you do not have to tell me that, but all this would be too much hard work for me. Especially with my knees. They creak like a great oak in a hurricane. Well, enough of my medical ailments, you do not want to hear about my collection of rashes, we could be here all day. HB

Chapter 28

They stood, dwarfed by the sheer size of the arched wooden studded door. It looked thick, solid and battle scarred. It was the perfect door for such a bulky rusted old key as the one in Perry's hand.

Malaika felt that this should have been more of a solemn experience, but with the hi-vis vests they wore and the additional hard hat she sported, it seemed more comical in nature.

Perry drove the large key into the doors' lock and with a bit of a struggle, and no little effort, he managed to unlock the beast. Perry was surprised at how easily it then opened, the horrible echoing screeching shriek he expected failed to report to duty, no doubt thanks to Grubbin's trusty oil can.

'So far so good,' smiled Perry, pleased with their progress to date. He aimed his torch inside, took a deep breath and stepped forwards.

Although referred to as the catacombs, a more fitting name was that of basement. Far duller, hardly exciting, but essentially that is what it was. They both entered and started down the well-worn stone steps.

SQUEAK... **SQUEAL...** CHEEP...

'What was that!' Shrieked Malaika, 'It's bats, I knew there would be bats down here. Perry, I don't think I can do this.'

'It's okay, just my shoes voicing their fear, that's all...'

'So, this could have been the dungeon, right? You know, back in the day.' The light from her torch was giving everything an eerie lustre.

'I guess so, it certainly goes down far enough, definitely part of the original castle foundations, that's for sure.'

Long shadows played along the walls as they made their descent, deeper and deeper until it opened into a large musty smelling room. They cast the lens of their torches around the cavern, surveying everything that emerged from the darkness. It currently held old mattresses piled high on top of each other, a tangle of broken three-legged chairs wrestling with each other in a corner, wardrobes missing doors and dignity, a variety of rolled up pieces of stained carpet and a small army of wilting cardboard boxes. This was the graveyard of old and forgotten hotel furniture, all covered with a shimmer of dust and cobwebs.

'Does your uncle never throw anything out?' asked Malaika as she tried to squeeze herself through an obstacle course of dilapidated drawers.

'Me and my family, quite soon as it happens,' sighed Perry.

'It's not going to come to that, certainly not after we've gone to all this effort.'

'I vaguely remember he once sent Grubbins on a carpentry course, but he got sent home the next day with a rather vicious splinter in his nose, I've no idea what he had been doing. To be fair my father ensures things don't get too shabby in the hotel, so a lot of this will be his work. He's probably forgotten just how much junk has been collected down here. Uncle Hugo also thinks this part of the hotel is haunted, so he is never down either.'

'So, who does come here then?'

'This is all Grubbins handywork. At one point all the wine was kept down here as well. Uncle Hugo would encourage him to experiment with it. Always thinking about the bar profit.

'This will do,' said Malaika coming to a stop. She pulled out her homemade map and laid it down on a rickety dusty table that was standing isolated and feeling somewhat sorry for itself.

'Okay, so we came in from here, walked about this far and took a slight turn.' She tapped the map with her finger. 'I think we are roughly here; we still have a lot of ground to cover, assuming we have full access of course.'

'And not in ideal circumstances,' added Perry, who looked over his shoulder into the gloom.

'We will be fine,' she said.

'What about those movies you mentioned.'

'As long as we don't split up,' she confirmed. 'Things always go downhill when you split up.'

'So how are we going to do this?' questioned Perry. 'There is a lot of rubbish down here and obviously you don't have your metal detector, which would have helped.'

'I was too busy rushing up here to make sure you were okay. Not worrying about metal detectors,' she snapped.

Silence hung in the room.

'I'm sorry,' he said.

'Apology accepted,' she replied. 'Look, we just need to make the best of things under the circumstances. With what's going on upstairs and outside this is a logical place to look first. It's all brick down here, old stone and masonry. If this is where the Plimsoll Bandit hid it, fingers crossed, he wouldn't have had that much time.

I can't imagine he would have dug a hole to bury it,' she continued. 'The walls perhaps, now that's a different matter. I think we should take a wall each. Go over it brick by brick. Look for anything loose or wobbly. Anything with cement around it that looks fresher than the rest of the stonework.'

There was a noise, like a muffled duck quack.

'Sssshh, did you hear that?

'Nothing, it was nothing,' Perry assured her.

'No, I heard something. It could be important. It was like a drowning duck.'

'I said leave it. It was nothing.'

'Oh... oh Perry, you didn't... not down here. Oh My! That really smells! How could you?'

'Apologies, I'm a little nervous.'

'Yeah, you and your shoes. Was it top or bottom?'

'It was a very small belch, I said I was sorry.'

'Well, if we survive this, the first thing you are doing is brushing your teeth.'

CLUNK-CLUNK

'Wait, what was that' said Malaika.

'Not again. It wasn't me. I didn't hear anything,' said Perry after a few seconds of silence.

'I did, I'm sure I did, it sounded like furniture moving.'

They both held their torches high and cast their beams this way and that, leaving no corner of the room unlit. Across the floor, along the walls, they even swept the ceiling.

'All clear,' said Perry, 'just us.'

'Sorry,' said Malaika, 'I'm getting jumpy.'

CLUNK-CLUNK

They both heard that, accompanied by a shadow moving on the wall, that they knew was not theirs. Someone was down here with them.

CLUNK-CLUNK

CLUNK-CLUNK

Then, as if things couldn't get any worse, the door above was slammed shut, with a deafening boom. The scraping turn of a key confirmed their worst fears. Somebody had locked them in. They were both trapped in this underground labyrinth.

Ah, the joys of playing around in the dark. If I had been there, I would have jumped out of one of the wardrobes. I did that to someone once. I even visited them in hospital afterwards to apologise. HB

Chapter 29

Now, what have we here? Why, two naughty children who should have been safe and sound in their beds. Instead, they are roaming and wandering around the hotel. Just what were they playing at?

It had heard them coming, their attempts at silence amateurish due to their constant talking and what sounded like a pet mouse squeaking. There was not enough time to hide, but it didn't need to, it already was, in plain sight.

Tentatively they approached, in their garish fluorescent attire, and attempted to move the obstacle out of the way. It was slightly undignified, but most amusing. They simply had no idea there was someone in the suit of armour, never mind who it was.

It then watched as they continued down the corridor before halting at an impressive wooden door which towered above them.

The boy with the messy hair was now toying with a large key, which he finally inserted into the lock. Soon he had the door open, and they both finally gathered the nerve to venture inside.

All very strange it thought, exactly what are they up to? It would be risky, dangerous perhaps. It had a plan after all. A timetable to be followed. But it was inquisitive. It needed to know what they were up to. It could not allow a pair of children to affect what was about to unfold. It followed them.

It did its best to lower itself into the room, step by step, but it would not be possible to follow them all the way down. Not without its own light and certainly not in its current guise. Instead, it focussed its attention on the noises below. It could hear them, they were talking and planning, the rustling of paper, it was a map. So that was it. They were treasure hunters, just silly childish games. It smiled to itself.

Then it gagged. What was that smell? As it fought for fresh air it brushed against the wall.

CLUNK-CLUNK

It cursed itself for being so sloppy. The children had noticed, they knew they were not alone. The silence stretched on, perhaps they would ignore it and continue with their planning. But no, they were waving their torches back and forth, looking for the source of the noise. It would be seen, it would be discovered, it needed to resolve the situation, to be on the front foot again. The decision was simple. It did its best to turn itself around on the step.

CLUNK-CLUNK

With stealth and secrecy now abandoned, the robust shape lumbered up the remaining stairs before they had the chance to act.

CLUNK-CLUNK

CLUNK-CLUNK

They had been caught unawares and it was already slamming the wooden door shut before they had even worked out what was happening.

With the great door now closed, the key was turned, the lock making a satisfying click. It allowed itself to take in gulps of sweet clean air. It needed to get upstairs, get back on schedule. As for them, they were trapped down there and at best would not be discovered until morning, if ever.

Little does this phantom watcher realise that I am watching them. Oh, the irony. Both of us, Peeping Toms. I do like to think I hold a moral high ground here I have to say. This is my job after all: well except for that incident last year, but the less said about that the better – in my defence, all charges were eventually dropped. HB

Chapter 30

'I'm... I'm not sure we should be doing this,' groaned Sorry Noakes. The candle in his hand was shaking. 'I mean, what if we run into him, around this corner, or the next. I've heard he's almost seven feet, a beast of a man, hands as big as shovels, hair like a lion's mane...'

'Who told you that,' laughed Jimmy James Jr. quietly.

'That... That barman, the one with the funny belly button.'

'Listen Sorry, life is an adventure and right now we are lucky to be living in what I am sure will be one of its most vibrant high points. So, no more negativity okay. I get up every morning and do my yoga to the music of whales singing and doves fluttering, to ensure I start the day with a positive mindset. Anyway, the fact of the matter is that no one would dare tussle with two tough hombres like us. I tell you Sorry, what happens tonight will be a tale we will be telling the grandkids about one day.'

'One... One day, grandkids,' repeated Sorry Noakes numbly, he was now feeling well and truly in over his head.

'Now, speaking of that strange Grubbins fellow, I slipped him a generous tip before we came up here and he told me all about that museum theft and the story about it being hidden here somewhere in the hotel. To be fair, he said he didn't believe it, but I guess after everything that's happened today, the joke is on him.'

'I... I don't think Mr Gentle-Me saw the funny side of things either,' said Sorry, who was still waving his candle around in a jerky, nervy manner.

'It was unfortunate to be sure, but he looked about 100 and had lived a full life, and then some. What we need to focus on is the simple fact that the strangler is only here because those pilfered crown jewels are here. If we can find them my friend, then we are rolling in the money. Did anyone mention the substantial reward to you? Now, when I say substantial, I mean MASSIVE.' Jimmy James Jr. gave another blinding smile.

CLUNK-CLUNK

'What... What was that, did you hear something?' said Sorry.

They both walked around the corner. Only one of them successfully made it however, as Sorry Noakes was catapulted back the way he had come. He landed on his back, arms and legs flailing.

'What... What was that?' he whimpered, slightly dazed.

Jimmy James Jr. stuck his head around the corner and looked down at him. 'You just walked into a suit of armour,' he confirmed. 'How did you not see it?'

'How... How did I not see it, I'll tell you how, because the last thing you expect, when walking around a corner, is for a suit of armour to jump out at you, especially when it wasn't there on the way up!'

Jimmy James Jr. helped him to his feet.

'Are you sure it wasn't here earlier? Hey, that looks like a new dent on it, I hope you don't get into any trouble.'

'Just... Just help me move it out of the way, stick it over there.'

With a lot of groaning and a great deal of exertion, they managed to shift the lump of dented metal up against the wall.

'That... That thing weighs a ton,' complained Sorry Noakes.

'It did indeed,' agreed Jimmy James Jr., who was huffing and puffing.

'Gee whiz,' he cried.

'What... What is it now?' squealed Sorry. He was ready to run back to his room and due to the weight of his feet he needed as much of a head start as possible.

'Look at this,' said Jimmy James Jr. who was holding up his candle and pointing to a painting of a man posing in what looked like a toga. The man was lying on a red velvet looking couch, perhaps originally trying to look cultured, perceptive, scholarly even. Alas the painter had only managed to capture a grim look of frightened constipation.

'What is it with this hotel and these bizarre paintings, they are everywhere. Look here, this fella is called Punctual. Punctual Bumbler! I hate to tell you this Sorry, but the people in your country are unhinged.' Jimmy James Jr. walked on.

'Look... Look, this treasure thingy, we don't know where it is,' said Sorry Noakes trying to get things back on track. 'I mean it could be anywhere, this place is massive, it's pitch black, we have no chance of finding it.'

'I agree, this is the proverbial lost sock of all treasures.'

'Don't... Don't say such a thing,' said a horrified Sorry Noakes.

It's okay, I'm not looking for the treasure exactly,' said Jimmy James Jr.

'You're... You're not,' said Sorry looking quite relieved. 'Does that mean we can go back to our rooms now? I have a thermos flask with my favourite hot chocolate. A nice little cup of that and an early night for me then. Fingers crossed I don't get strangled in my sleep obviously and then first thing in the morning, I'm checking out of this ghastly place.'

'Well, to clarify, I'm not looking for the treasure as such. This is like nature at work. Whoever has the treasure is the prey and we, my friend, need to become the predators.'

'No... No, you have quite lost me I'm afraid.'

'I have a philosophy I live my life by Sorry. Once when I was out surfing, I had a little accident and when I washed up on shore, lucky to be alive, there next to me was a wise turtle. He whispered in my ear and what he said changed the course of my life. I can't tell you what exactly, that could fill an entire book, but when I face challenges in life, I just ask myself - *What Would The Turtle Do?*

So, I agree with you, it's pointless trying to look for the treasure, it's been too well hidden all these years. No, there is a far simpler and more effective way of finding it. We, Mr Noakes are not looking for the treasure as such, we are instead looking for the strangler, who will have the treasure in his possession. Find him, find the crown jewels. Simple. It's what the turtle would do.'

'Are... Are you mad,' cried Sorry, 'you want to FIND the strangler!' He had to put his hand up against the wall to steady himself, his knees once again about to give up on him. His heart was beating too fast, and he could feel the hysteria building up inside him.

'Deep breaths, Sorry, deep breaths. That's it. I really don't want to see that little friend of yours again. But don't worry, there is one of him and two of us, plus I also have this,' and with a flick of his wrist his spork once again appeared in his hand as if by sorcery.

'What... What am I doing,' questioned Sorry Noakes to himself, looking close to tears. 'I'm out hunting a dangerous murderer in a creepy unlit hotel. I apparently have gangrenous feet and I'm partnered with a turtle talking amateur magician, who is waving a little plastic spoon about like it's King Arthur's sword. Listen, I'm going back to my room, I don't care about any reward money.'

'Hey, calm down, calm down. You'll be safe with me here, nothing will go...'

Both their candles blew out.

Sorry Noakes gave a cry so high in pitch no human could hear it. Unfortunately, it did wake up poor Pretzel, who had been sleeping contentedly in Erstwhile's office, after having enjoyed a rather considerable, if not overcooked, chicken dinner.

Sorry frantically fumbled in his pocket, he had a lighter somewhere. He didn't smoke, it was a filthy habit, but if a customer did, he was only too happy to offer them a light. His fingers slithered around hunting for it, knowing that with every passing second a giant pair of hands might clamp around his neck. Finally, he found what he was looking for and with trembling hands pulled it out and managed to relight his candle.

'Give me your candle,' he called to Jimmy James Jr., but there was no reply. Sorry Noakes raised his candle high and looked up and down the corridor. He swivelled left then right, or was it East then West, might even have been North then South, but he was gone. Aside from an unpleasant long blonde hair that clung to his sleeve, Jimmy James Jr. was nowhere to be seen. He had vanished.

Look out Criminals and Ne'er-do-wells, there is a new dynamic duo in town. Oh, woe is me. I think someone needs to explain to Jimmy James Jr. that the turtle, if not stuck on its back, would be scurrying off home as quickly as possible. HB

Chapter 31

They tried the door, knowing full well it was locked, with the key on the other side and they were not to be disappointed. They then resorted to banging on the door, kicking the door, yelling at the door... but nothing. Dejected, they both stumbled back downstairs into the chamber to look for another way out.

'We are walking in circles,' said Perry after about 10 minutes.

'Are we, I'm not sure,' said Malaika. She was loath to admit it, but her usually bang on sense of direction seemed to have deserted her.

'Yeah, we definitely are,' said Perry, he shone his torch on a wardrobe that was sporting a sticker of a bunny rabbit. 'I've passed this at least once already.'

'Okay, we need to shake things up a little. How about we split up,' she suggested.

'But I thought you said bad things happen when you go it alone?'

'Well, technically, but it can't get much worse, can it? On the downside we are trapped here, but on the plus side the strangler isn't. He is on the other side of that locked door.'

'You really think it was him?' gulped Perry.

'I can't think of who else would do this to us,' sighed Malaika. 'I'm afraid to say it also means that the stolen museum treasure is very unlikely to be down here.'

Malaika could sense Perry deflate.

'Look, it's fine,' she said, 'we can't worry about that right now, we need to focus on getting out of here. So, lets split up and take our chances. How about I go left, and you go right.'

Neither choice looked particularly attractive, but Perry agreed. Malaika was correct, they needed to take charge of the situation.

Perry continued down the corridor, the fact he was having to wipe away the odd cobweb from his face at least gave him the confidence it was a route so far unexplored. It stretched on and on and then split into two directions He ended up trying them both as ultimately, they led to dead ends. He was hoping that Malaika was having better luck than him - when the world fell in.

BOOOOOOOOOOOOO OOOOOOOOOOOMM MMMMMMMMM!

An almighty explosion rocked everything. A great booming from above which caused dust and dirt to rain down upon him. Perry brought out a handkerchief which he used to cover his mouth. He could hardly breathe, and the dust cloud made the limited visibility even worse. Coughing with every step he took, he hoped he was walking back the way he had come for he was desperate to find Malaika.

It took him longer than expected but he eventually found himself at the point where they had agreed to split up. If he continued, then he would hopefully catch up with her, but Perry was horrified to see that the path Malaika had followed was no longer there.

A section of the ceiling had collapsed. Massive rocks and boulders had piled down upon themselves completely blocking the corridor. Malaika was somewhere on the other side of this rubble. She was trapped and maybe hurt.

Good old unexpected cave ins and their dusty aftermath. A handy face mask is another in a long list of excellent uses for a scarf. Along with a makeshift belt. A swing to traverse a pit of snakes. A starters flag for an impromptu illegal street race. A turban for a fancy dress party. A hammock for vertically challenged people. A lasso when wombat hunting. Needless to say, I never leave home without one. HB

Chapter 32

The hotel shook. It literally shuddered. Then the belated sound of the explosion...

BOOOOOOOOOOOOO OOOOOOOOOOOOMM MMMMMMMMM!

Followed by silence...

'That was not the weather,' shouted Erstwhile to Grubbins, 'come on, it came from somewhere below.'

As they ran downstairs and through the corridors, they clattered into Sorry Noakes, who was sent sprawling.

'Not... Not again,' he wailed. What was that noise?'

'No idea, but you better come with us and find out,' replied Erstwhile as he set off again.

The three of them finally arrived at reception, where plumes of black smoke were belching out of the dining room, via the kitchen. When they reached it, they found none other than Jimmy James Jr. with a fire extinguisher in hand, blasting at everything and anything.

'What - on - Earth?' spluttered Hugo who had just joined the party.

'Honestly, I've no idea,' replied Erstwhile, trying his best to waft away the smoke and fire extinguisher powder.

'I think it was a gas leak,' said Jimmy James Jr. who then broke into a round of coughing. He was standing next to what was left of the destroyed stove. 'Probably one of the candles around here was still lit. We were lucky, it must have been a slow leak, or it could have taken out the entire side of the hotel.

'Oh my,' was all Hugo could muster, looking at the carnage. The blackened walls and parts of the kitchen still smouldering.

'What... What happened to you upstairs, you just vanished and left me,' Sorry quietly asked Jimmy James Jr.

'I thought I heard something. Do you remember what I said? The turtle is free, the turtle is fluid, be the turtle, swim to your destiny...'

'No... No thanks old bean, I would rather be the hedgehog, and right now I want to curl up into a ball until morning time.'

CLUNK-CLUNK

Everyone began looking around the room.

CLUNK-CLUNK

'The... The hotel is collapsing,' muttered Sorry Noakes.

CLUNK-CLUNK

'No, it's the pipes, the water pipes, the central heating,' said Hugo.

CLUNK-CLUNK

'It might also be the gas pipe,' cautioned Erstwhile. He looked towards Grubbins who was already in motion.

'I'll make sure the main supply is shut off sir,' as he shuffled towards the exit. Hugo however was in a foul mood and couldn't help himself.

'Grubbins! It's well understood this hotel is passed down through the generations, but is it the same practice with those shoes of yours? Look at the state of them! When was the last time you even cleaned them?'

'I think it was the last time you had something nice to say,' he replied, looking down at his admittedly distressed footwear.

'What! You impertinent pleb, how dare you,' Hugo's wobbly cheeks were burning crimson.

'Thank you M'lud.'

Sorry Noakes smiled to himself. There had been a slight odour around that Grubbins fellow and now he could put his finger on it. It was like crusty old socks, recently retired after years of daily service. It made his heart soar.

'What a night,' said an embarrassed Hugo who kicked a blackened piece of debris across the floor. 'What more can go wrong?'

'It was only a matter of time Hugo; I did try to warn you. Too many guests have suffered from the work carried out in this evil place. Eventually there had to be retribution,' said Erstwhile gravely.

'It might not have been deliberate; do you remember that time we asked her to prepare an eight-course meal? The whole kitchen had to be remodelled after that.'

'You... You don't think this was an accident, do you?' squeaked Sorry Noakes. 'It was him, the strangler. He was trying to kill us all, at once, rather than doing it individually.'

'I hate to admit it, but he makes a good point,' said Erstwhile. 'With everything that's happened today, this can't just be a coincidence. Besides, I'm positive all the candles were extinguished before we moved everyone upstairs.'

'What... What's that?' said Sorry, 'I heard something.'

'Probably just aftershocks, with an old building like this there could be structural damage,' suggested Jimmy James Jr.

'No, wait, I think I hear it too,' said Erstwhile, tilting his head.

'Could someone be in trouble?' questioned Jimmy James Jr.

They hurriedly left the smoking wreck of the kitchen and stepped into the dining room.

'Our only hope of getting out of this is if Belinda gets her hands on the culprit first. She will be livid,' mumbled Hugo.

'Over here, there is definitely a sound,' said Erstwhile as he led them into reception.

'What is that doing there?' he questioned. He was referring to the suit of armour, which was standing in the centre of the room.

'Yes... Yes, these things do tend to pop out at you, I'm glad I'm not the only one who's noticed,' exclaimed Sorry Noakes.

'Maybe it was those aftershocks, the long-haired fellow was talking about, but who cares, it's there now, so get it moved back to its usual place next to the door,' grumbled Hugo.

With a lot of whimpering, and a significant amount of industry, Erstwhile single handedly managed to manoeuvre the lump of Bumbler history back into its usual spot, next to the main entrance.

'That thing weighs a ton,' he said wearily.

'You're out of shape brother,' remarked Hugo, sucking his stomach in.

'I... I can hear it again, is that coming from upstairs?' said Sorry.

'No, I think that's downstairs, it sounds like it's under us,' replied Erstwhile.'

'And what's downstairs?' asked Jimmy James Jr.

'Just a few rooms for supplies and a basement for storing old bric-a-brac,' said Hugo, 'and maybe a ghost...,' although he whispered that part to himself.

Erstwhile guided everyone through a corridor, to the right of the reception steps, past the hotel washrooms and then down a secluded set of fire stairs. Soon they were standing in a short corridor, where a muffled noise could be heard from behind a grand old wooden door. It was now a feeble thumping.

'Someone is in there,' said Hugo, stating the obvious.

'Well, lets find out,' said Erstwhile. The key was still in the lock, which was another question that needed answering. He turned the key and was shocked when Perry almost fell into his arms.

Perry had tears in his eyes as he hugged his father tightly.

'What are you doing down here? You should be in your room.' He was too shocked to be angry.

'Never mind that dad, it's Malaika.'

'What about her?'

'We were down there, down in the catacombs. We were looking about and then there was a bang, everything shook, the ceiling collapsed dad. Malaika was on the other side of it, she's trapped.'

'Gee whiz,' gasped Jimmy James Jr.

Perry's dad started organising things. He replaced the candle he was holding with the flashlight that Perry held.

'Mr James, I can't make you, but I would be very grateful if you would come down with me.' Jimmy James Jr. nodded in agreement. 'The rest of you stay here, it may be unsafe down there.'

'Young... Young man,' said Sorry Noakes, 'why don't we go upstairs and find some fizzy pop. You look like you could do with some.'

Perry shook his head. 'If it's okay Mr Noakes, I'll stay here. I need to know how my friend is.'

'I'll go up with you.' said Uncle Hugo, as insensitive as always. 'That smoke has parched my throat, and it will take something stronger that fizzy pop to quench it.'

Both Perry and Sorry ignored him as they watched Perry's father and Jimmy James Jr. take tentative steps down into the gloom.

Eventually they both made their winding way to the pile of wreckage that blocked the corridor. Erstwhile tried removing some of the larger stones that barred their way, but more just fell in to replace them.

'Okay,' he said stopping, 'I don't want to make this any worse than it already is. We'll need to wait until help arrives.'

'If it arrives,' said Jimmy James Jr. ominously. He was squatting low to avoid hitting his head and potentially causing even more damage.

'Hello...,' came a faint voice from behind the mound of ruins.

'Malaika? Is that you,' shouted Erstwhile with a grin on his face. 'It's me, Perry's dad, can you hear me? Are you okay?'

'Yes, thank you,' came the distant voice. 'Something hit me on the head. I think I blacked out. Lucky I was wearing this hard hat, but I'm fine now.'

'That's good, really good,' he said. 'Listen, we can't move this rubble at the moment. I'm scared we will make things worse.'

'I understand,' said Malaika.

'You are very brave,' said Erstwhile. 'There was an explosion in the kitchen, that's what's caused all this.'

'Is everyone okay? Is Perry okay?'

'He's fine, I think everyone is fine, but we still have a few people to round up, we'll do that soon. Can I just ask, what is it like on your side of this mess?'

'Oh, I have plenty of space, a wall has fallen down, I might be able to crawl through it and see where it takes me.'

'You better not, it could be dangerous. Listen, we are going to go upstairs now and make sure everyone else is okay, and then I'm heading down to the village to summon help... somehow.'

What would the heroic HB have done in this situation? A very good question. Being a fan of 1980's action movies, I feel there could be only one outcome. The music would ramp up, as I remove my hat, scarf, and coat. There would then follow an extended montage of me flashing my oiled and shiny abs and other buff body parts. I keep myself in great physical shape for a man of my years, you will just have to take my word for that. The rescue would then go to plan, and I would sign off with a pithy one liner that takes everyone's breath away. A usual Thursday for me then. HB

Chapter 33

'She's okay,' said Perry's dusty looking father as he came back up through the heavy wooden door. Perry gave a huge sigh of relief. 'We can't dig her out though, we are going to need professional help, which I'm going to get.'

'Exactly how?' asked Uncle Hugo.

'I've no choice, I need to get down to the village. There must be some part of the river that can be crossed, but first we need to make sure everyone else is okay. We need to get everyone in the drawing room. Strength in numbers and all that.'

doom...
doom...
doom...

'What... What now?' whispered Sorry.

'Is someone else trapped?' gasped Jimmy James Jr.

'No, it's the door,' said Perry, 'the front door is locked.'

'Someone is at the door,' said Uncle Hugo, he couldn't believe the words he was saying. It didn't sound possible.

They climbed up the stairs to reception and slowly approached the hotel entrance, just in time for another round of

doom...

doom...

doom...

Perry's dad reached out to open the door.

'Now steady on there, aren't you going to ask who is out there? In this storm, with the bridge all gone, it can't be anyone from the village. It could be the strangler himself for all we know.' Jimmy James Jr. was nervously playing with the overlarge lapels of his suit.

'Unlikely.'

'Maybe, but no harm in asking.'

Perry's father nodded, he pressed himself up against the door and shouted 'WHO IS IT? IDENTIFY YOURSELF.'

There was a muffled reply, but the wind and rain drowned it out.

'Well, what did they say?' asked Uncle Hugo.

'I couldn't hear, I couldn't make it out.'

'Just open it dad,' gulped Perry as he gripped his candle tightly. Uncle Hugo gave him a rather dirty look. Sorry Noakes then wandered off looking for another chair, as if he was some form of lion tamer. Meanwhile, with a flick of his wrist, Jimmy James Jr. had conjured up another small spork, which he was waving about threateningly.

'Okay, here we go,' said Perry's dad. He turned the key in the lock and undid the bolts at the top and bottom of the door. 'Watch your candles everyone.' He took a breath then flung the door open, mostly assisted by the squall outside. 'Oh my,' he cried...

There, standing at the door, soaking wet and shivering was a portly man in nothing but a string vest and underwear.

'What is that!' said Jimmy James Jr., his eyes wide in surprise, of all the things he thought may have been behind the door, this was not one of them.

'Who... Who is that?' said Sorry Noakes, from his safe vantage point behind the chair, looking at what could only be described as some form of extreme sunbather.

'This,' said Perry's father smiling, 'is none other than Sergeant McSweeney. It's the police.'

As Uncle Hugo fought to close and relock the door, the rest of them helped guide, half carry, the almost blue Sergeant into the drawing room. All except for Grubbins, who had returned and was already mopping up the pools of water that were gathering on the floor.

Job done, the mercurial Grubbins then produced a flask from somewhere, poured and handed the shivering Sergeant a steaming cup of coffee.

'That's a good idea Grubbins,' said Perry's dad. 'If I remember rightly there is an old camping stove lying around which we could use. Assuming she is over the shock of what's happened to the kitchen, could you ask Belinda to have a look for it and rustle up some hot drinks for everyone.'

Grubbins gave a salute and started to head off. Uncle Hugo spotted something, however.

'Grubbins! What's that around your neck? Are you wearing a garland of... sprouts! What are you up to?'

'For protection M'lud. Against the strangler.

If eye-rolling could ever be monetised, Uncle Hugo would be the one rolling, in filthy lucre.

'These sprouts could stop an elephant M'lud.'

'Listen, you uneducated, unenlightened, empty-headed, feeble-minded, superstitious peasant. This is no longer the Middle Ages, regardless of how you dress. Has everyone taken a leave of their senses? Take it off, off at once and bring those hot drinks back. He's not a vampire you know.'

'It's garlic M'lud. It's garlic that vampires are scared of,' announced Grubbins as he shuffled off.

The humiliation on his uncle's face was well deserved. Perry longed to deliver a swift kick to his shins as the Coup de grâce. Despite the days events his uncle was still trying to belittle everyone. Grubbins and Belinda were lovely people, they deserved better than this. His chain of thought turned and twisted in his head, reminding him of his shortcomings, not least his absolute failure in saving the hotel.

They stood around the shaking Sergeant who was gulping down his drink. At least his skin was slowly starting to turn a more pinkish colour. Soon some towels were found to help dry him and protect his modesty. Uncle Hugo was about to ask him something, but Perry's father held up his hand.

'He'll speak when he's able.'

'I can't believe it's just him though,' Uncle Hugo continued regardless. 'And where is his uniform? Is he undercover? Perry's dad rolled his eyes.

'Hey, who cares, you said he's a cop and that's just swell,' said Jimmy James Jr. 'The cavalry has arrived, but where's his gun?'

The... The police are not armed in our country old bean,' Sorry informed him. 'This is not the wild west you know. They usually carry a little wooden stick called a truncheon.'

'A truncheon...,' Jimmy James Jr. chewed on the word. 'Okay, so where is his little wooden truncheon thing?'

'He was probably mugged, yes, I bet that's what happened, they took everything and thankfully, for us, left him with his underwear.' Uncle Hugo now seemed to be feeling slightly better about his kilt incident of earlier.

'Please, more,' gasped the trembling Sergeant who lifted his empty cup into the air. Perry was quick to refill it with the last dregs from the flask. The Sergeant drank the steaming liquid in one.

Sorry Noakes seemed quite impressed, as if this was on a par with swallowing a flaming sword.

The Sergeant's incessant shivering was now beginning to ease off, but the growing puddle of water beneath his chair was growing larger.

'Right,' he finally spoke, placing the empty cup in the puddle with a splash. 'Right,' he said again as he stared intently at everyone. 'I almost got maself killed getting here tonight. We got a call at the station. It said there had been a death. The constable who took the call also said the word '**murder**' was used. Well, I swear, there will be murder here tonight if this has all been a hoax.'

I am feeling wet, cold and miserable just reading this. I am of course just referring to this chapter, keep your caustic comments on the whole book to yourself. Achoo. HB

Chapter 34

Jimmy James Jr. quickly held up his hand. 'What did he say, I didn't catch it all, what language is he speaking?'

The Sergeant turned to him, 'I'm Scottish laddie, ye got a problem with that?'

The room fell into an awkward silence.

'Nope, I didn't understand that either, it must be the cold, it's numbed his tongue, we need more coffee over here,' he shouted.

Perry caught his faint smell of suntan lotion and minty toothpaste, just as everyone then tried to speak at once.

'Sergeant,' shouted Perry's father loudly above the others, 'we are so relieved to have you here. There is so much to fill you in on but try and get your strength back and some heat in you. Please tell us though, what happened to you, are any of your men out there?'

The Sergeant shuddered at the thought of reliving it all again, but he wrapped the towels around him tightly and began his sombre tale.

'Originally there was three o' us headed over here, but we only got as far as the bridge. If ye didn't know, it's gone, completely washed away. The hotel is stranded. Well, I won't lie we were stumped, but one o' the constables had a wee idea. He knew about an old boat; people sometimes used it for a bit o' fishing. Despite the weather, we managed to retrieve it, but the river. Never in all ma days have I ever seen it like that. Fierce it was, fierce. But murder is a serious business, especially if others are still in danger, so we had no choice, we attempted to cross.

Ma poor two constables were rowing like madmen, but it was no good, we were drifting further and further down the river in the opposite direction. Then something hit the boat, I'm no sure what. I was catapulted into the water. It was a frenzy; I was upside down and tossed this way and that. I have no idea how I made it to the other side, but there I was, thankfully climbing and clawing maself up the riverbank. By now the rowing boat looked like it was miles away and they were both waving goodbye to me as they disappeared out o' sight. They should be fine though.

I then had to walk through the forest to get here, but as ye can see, the river stripped everything from me. Ma uniform, boots, walkie talkie, even ma handcuffs. I avoided drowning, but I thought I would freeze to death on the way over here, but somehow, I made it, I made it,' he groaned.

The Sergeant stood up on shaky legs and despite the volume of towels that swathed him, water was still dripping everywhere.

'Now, what exactly is going on around here?' He then began fanning his hand back and forth. 'Ye God's, having a wee problem with the drains are ye, no surprising in this weather.' He then gave a dry retch.

Sorry Noakes was about to say something, but Jimmy James Jr. put a hand on his shoulder to ensure his silence.

Perry's father quickly jumped in and did all the talking, to avoid everyone else from confusing matters. The Sergeant sat down again and listened intently. Perry's dad explained how they had uncovered the dead body of the unfortunate Mr Gentle-Me. Their fear that it may have been a murder. The attempt at calling the police station, just as the phone lines were cut. Then the horrific news of the Sopwith Strangler, who was on the loose and was heading here. To them it confirmed it had been a murder and if that alone was not enough to convince them that the mad strangler was lurking in their midst's, then surely the explosion in the kitchen settled it. He then wrapped up his summary of the day's events with news of the cave-in downstairs and the trapped Malaika.

'Jings, this is most alarming I have to say,' cried the Sergeant pressing himself into action. 'I can have a wee look at the body later, but there is something you need to hear right now. I'm happy to confirm that the Sopwith Strangler is not sneaking about the High Hill Hotel. I'm afraid to say we did indeed have some problems with our computers earlier today, a bit embarrassing, but thankfully due to Malaika's mother, o' she is wonderful you know, she fixed them all up. I never saw anything like it, she stripped them computers all down, rebuilt the hard drives, put on some antivirus software and before you know it, we were back in business.

Now, it turns out our police colleagues were still following the Sopwith Strangler and he didn't end up here in Little Didwob. No, it was another village a couple of miles away. They arrested him for grave robbing of all things. They thought it was the museum treasure he was looking for, but if so, it wasn't there. He's in police custody now, so if there has been a murder here, you can certainly rule him out.'

Sorry Noakes slumped down on to the floor, crossed his legs and began rocking back and forth, moaning slightly to himself.

'Just ignore him Sergeant, he has his own way of dealing with things,' said Perry's father.

'I... I have a condition don't you know,' Sorry limply replied, for some reason his glasses had now all steamed up.

'Well, the first order o' things is to get downstairs sharpish, we need to make sure that wee lass Malaika is still okay. Unfortunately, there's no much we can do without risking another cave in. Help will be here in the morning, I have no doubt, but that's still hours away. When was the last time ye heard from her?'

'Just before you arrived.'

'Good, but I want to go down and assess the situation for maself, her safety is paramount.'

Perry's dad and the towel laden Sergeant were just making their way out of the drawing room when they were both stopped in their tracks.

'I say,' said Mr Seymour Gentle-Me in a very raspy voice, 'what was that banging earlier, it woke me up? Is it time for breakfast yet?'

———●◎●———

A likely story – the river stole my clothes! That was the sort of ridiculous reporting that would usually feature on the front page of the short lived Didwob Sunday Sport. I remember one story being dedicated to a local missing shopping trolly that was discovered in North Korea. The rascals never did send it back. HB

Chapter 35

'**AAAAIIIIIEEEEE....,**' Uncle Hugo gave a blood curdling scream, the colour draining from his face.

'It's a zombie!' he continued before running and jumping on to the soggy Sergeants back. 'Save me officer, it's come for me. It's going to eat my brain. I deserve it, but... but you must save me. **PLEASE.'**

Everyone in the room was stunned, not just at Uncle Hugo's erratic behaviour, but the fact that he was technically correct. There, standing right there, at the doorway of the drawing room was the walking, talking, dead body of Mr Gentle-Me. He had indeed risen from the grave (or at least his bed) and had stumbled downstairs on corpse legs for a hearty breakfast of human brains.

Perry noticed that Sorry Noakes had toppled over from his sitting position into dead faint on the floor. Jimmy James Jr., eyes wide in panic, had backed himself into a corner and was attempting to make a cross from his spork and a finger.

In the background, Perry saw Grubbins, who had been heading towards the drawing room with a silver tray full of coffee and tea, notice the reanimated Mr Gentle-Me, turn about on his heels and scurry over to the reception desk which he hid behind.

'I... I... don't understand?' said Perry's dad who was looking at the others for help. 'I... I... mean, we checked, we checked him. He was dead.' He began rubbing his bald spot in puzzlement.

'Hang on, hang on one blinking minute,' said the Sergeant who was now beginning to understand the situation unfolding before him. He was not impressed. 'THIS is the murder victim?'

The fact that Uncle Hugo was hanging on to his back like a limpet didn't seem to phase the Sergeant, such was the rising tide of anger that was starting to build inside him.

'What's been going on down here?' croaked Mr Gentle-Me. 'Why are you all acting so strange?' He pointed to the rosy cheeked Sergeant 'who are you and why are you dripping wet in your underwear? Why is it still so dark around here? Why is Mr Noakes sleeping on the floor?' He touched his neck, 'Oh my throat, I must have been snoring like a bear last night, I do apologise if I kept anyone awake. Is that why Mr Noakes is having a cat nap?'

'Mr Gentle-Me, are you okay?' asked Perry, who put his dread of zombies to one side. He tried not to smile but he was so delighted to see the old man alive. He reached out and gently prodded him in the shoulder just in case it was some form of mass hallucination.

'We last saw you at lunch time. When you didn't come down for dinner, we came up to your room to make sure you were okay. That's when we found you, dead...'

'Dead...,' laughed Mr Gentle-Me, which then turned into a hacking cough. 'Dead! Do I look dead? No, don't answer that, I'm not at my best first thing in the morning.'

'Then we saw suspicious marks on your neck,' continued Perry's dad, 'we honestly thought you had been strangled. We couldn't wake you up. We couldn't find a pulse.'

Mr Gentle-Me ran his finger behind the maroon cravat he now wore. 'It is a bit sore I will admit,' he said hoarsely.

'Over here, let me have a look,' grumbled the Sergeant.

Despite the fact the ashen faced Uncle Hugo was still quivering on his back, the Sergeant examined Mr Gentle-Me's neck.

'Well, ye may be on to something,' he begrudgingly admitted as he squinted in the poor candlelight. 'There are bruises here, that's for sure and they could well be due to finger marks. I'm afraid to say that Mr Bumbler here could well be correct. Not in yer murder of course,' he gave Perry's dad a scornful side look, 'but I have to say it very much looks like someone did give it their very best try.'

Mr Gentle-Me was surprised and taken aback by the Sergeants admission.

'I'm a heavy sleeper, I'll admit that, it's one of the tricks of the trade when you are out on the road selling. You grab sleep on the fly, wherever and whenever you can, just like Mr Noakes here is demonstrating. Why, there was one time out in the Middle East I even slept on a bed of nails. It was an excellent sleep. I thought there would be a big market in nail beds over here, it was not to be however, I lost a packet on that venture.

I have to say though, snoozing through your own murder! Well, that's a new one, even for me. So, I guess the question is, which one of my esteemed colleagues wanted me out of the way, and why?'

'A very good question,' agreed the Sergeant, 'but before we get into all that we need to go down and ...'

'Looky. . . Looky. . . Looky. . .'

A shrieking voice filled the room. The Sergeant jumped back in shock. The passed out Sorry Noakes had raised his arm in the air and Mr Frock was back in the room.

'Oh, a puppet show,' smiled Mr Gentle-Me. 'I am warming to this man. I love a good puppet show.'

'He's a zombie he is. . . Keep your distance you rotting fiend. . . I don't have any brains for you. . . For that matter neither does that Hugo BUMbler. . . The boy though. . . You might get a snack out of him. . .'

Uncle Hugo had a face like thunder, while Perry just wanted to run.

'Ha Ha Ha,' laughed Mr Gentle-Me who instantly regretted it and grasped his throat. 'That wasn't wise,' he groaned. 'I...'

But before Mr Gentle-Me could say anything else, a haunting sound filled the room...

badoom...

badoom...

badoom...

I have encountered many a zombie in my time. In fact, I once chronicled it in my best seller entitled, 'My Many Encounters with a Zombie.' It is sadly out of print now, but if I do say so myself, it is a riveting read. Not to give too much away, it is full of zombies and the many times I have encountered them – what can I say. In this case however, he technically is not a zombie. Not to be nit–picky but being a sound sleeper does not one a zombie make. Even if you were fortunate enough to also sleepwalk and have a craving for people's brains. Sorry, I do not make the rules. HB

Chapter 36

badoom...
badoom...
badoom...

'Is... Is that the door again?' moaned Sorry Noakes, who had just woken up and was struggling to his feet. He then noticed Mr Gentle-Me standing there and his legs gave a little wobble. Jimmy James Jr. was now beside him and helped him remain steady.

'No,' said Perry's father, 'whatever it is, it's not coming from the door.'

It sounds like it's coming from... inside here,' volunteered Perry.

Everyone began spinning their heads looking around for the source of this phantom noise.

badoom...

badoom...

badoom...

Uncle Hugo's eyes bulged in alarm; they were surrounded in dark circles on a waxy face. He slid down from the back of the Sergeant and knelt on the floor as if in prayer and he began muttering to himself.

'The ghost... the ghost of the hotel had finally come for me... it knows what I have done... it has judged me unworthy... it has come to punish me...'

Everyone stepped away from Uncle Hugo who, with every passing second, was looking more and more unhinged. Perry was concerned that his uncle was on the cusp of a nervous breakdown, especially as he had now started frothing at the mouth.

'It's... it's breaking down the veil... the one between their paranormal world and ours... it's coming for me... to deliver a punishment... a terrible, terrible retribution. Sergeant, Sergeant... you must get me out of here.'

He had crawled over to the feet of the bemused police officer, who was now dripping water onto Uncle Hugo's head.

Everyone's attention was then torn from the embarrassing behaviour of Uncle Hugo as a series of barks and scratching filled the room.

'It's Pretzel,' confirmed Perry, 'he must have gotten out of the office.'

The hairy little dog seemed obsessed with part of the wall next to the fireplace. He barked again and began frantically scratching at the wallpaper as if his life depended on it.

'Maybe that's where the noise is coming from,' suggested Jimmy James Jr.

badoom...

badoom...

badoom...

'Yes,' he confirmed, 'it's coming from here.'

He joined Pretzel and began banging on the wall. Again and again, he banged with his fist and received three bangs in return.

'I think there is something behind the wall,' he cried.

'Of course,' shouted Perry. 'It's not something, it's someone. It's Malaika, it has to be, she found a way out.'

They all crowded around the fireplace, unsure what to do next.

'There is only one thing for it,' rumbled the Sergeant.

'Out of the way,' screamed Grubbins, who had appeared from nowhere. He was hefting a vicious looking pickaxe that certainly motivated everyone to scatter. He stopped and swung it with force at the wall.

'That's the spirit,' roared the Sergeant. 'If that's Malaika behind the wall, stand back, we are coming to get ye. That goes for us as well.' He motioned everyone to move further back out of the way of Grubbins and his energetic swings. Everyone that is bar Pretzel, who was still bidding his own mini rescue attempt further down the wall.

Again, and again and again Grubbins struck at the wall and eventually brick, and plaster started to rain down on to the floor. Pretzel got the message at that point and backed away. Soon enough, everyone had gathered again and was helping to wrestle parts of the wall loose, tearing at everything they could until a rough hole began to appear. Suddenly a horrifying face filled the void.

'Boy, am I glad to see you all,' coughed Malakai who pulled off the now filthy mask Grubbins had lent her earlier. Everyone gave a cheer and on they continued, ripping, kicking, and pulling until they had a space big enough to pull her out. She was clutching a wooden chest in her arms.

'Are you okay?' said Perry, who gave her a big hug despite the coating of cobwebs she had accumulated.

'I won't lie, it looked grim for a while, but after talking to your dad I calmed down. While I waited for a rescue, I thought there would be no harm in having a little look at what lay on my side of the cave in. When the ceiling fell it also opened a hole in one of the walls, it led to some form of passage. I followed it, I was careful, but I still got lost, eventually I could hear voices. It was all of you. I traced the noise straight to the wall and started banging. Then I heard this little beauty start to bark and scratch.' She reached down and gave Pretzel a big scratch of his own behind his ear.

'Well, that seems to be two of our problems sorted then,' said the Sergeant relieved.

'Sergeant McSweeney is that you?' asked Malaika. 'Why are you dressed in a toga? And what's the other problem?' she whispered to Perry.

'Malaika, can I introduce you to Mr Gentle-Me,' said Perry motioning towards the old man standing in the room.

Malaika gave a strangled cry. 'I thought he was....'

'Yes,' said Perry interjecting, 'it looks like we were a little off with that, he's just a heavy sleeper. Someone here did try to kill him though, and it was not the Sopwith Strangler.'

Malaika's eyebrows shot up.

'Yup, Sergeant McSweeney confirmed he was arrested earlier today, in a different village altogether.'

'Well, well, well,' said Malaika trying to make sense of all the revelations.

'Just to confirm, you will be paying for the damage caused,' uttered the voice of Uncle Hugo. He seemed to have recovered from his little meltdown of earlier, as if it had never happened. His abject look of fear had been replaced by anger and now.... curiousness.

'What's that you have there girl? In that box.'

'This is not the time and place Hugo,' said Perry's dad crossly.

Perry smiled; it was nice to see his father stand up to his brother.

Malaika held up the dust covered box in the dim light.

'This little beauty fell on my head after the explosion. Just as well I was wearing that silly hat eh.'

Horatio BLOOM

Uncle Hugo's face emitted a sour look when he realised what she had been wearing, and where it must have originated from.

'I'm not sure what's in it though. It looks really old, and the lock is rusted over, I've not been able to open it.'

'Could it be...,' started Perry, eyes widening.

'Treasure...,' finished Uncle Hugo, eyes bulging. 'Found in MY hotel, therefore MY property,' his eyes glazed over with greed. He tried to snatch the box from her, but Malaika was far too quick and easily pulled it out of reach of his chubby digits.

'Sergeant,' commanded Uncle Hugo, 'I demand you seize that box and open it.'

'Oh, do ye now,' replied the Sergeant, his face reddening in anger.

Malaika, however, handed him the wooden box to try and defuse the situation.

'Get that box open Sergeant, that treasure is mine,' Uncle Hugo snapped.

The Sergeant humoured him and examined the box from a variety of angles, the lock was indeed rusted over, it would take some force. Grubbins, almost reading his mind, handed over his pickaxe to him which the Sergeant accepted.

He placed the dirty, dusty wooden box on a table, raised the pickaxe, and with a careful and precise aim struck the lock with it. And again. And again. Finally, the fragments of rusted metal fell on to the table, the lock was broken. Much to the annoyance of Uncle Hugo, the Sergeant gestured for Malaika to open the box.

'**Looky**... **Looky**... **Looky**...'

Came the chilling voice that froze everyone.

'Oooh... It better not be a box of musty medieval sprouts... Mr Frock would get ANGREE... You wouldn't like Mr Frock when he is ANGREE...'

The room fell into silence, as everyone did their best to ignore what had just occurred.

Malaika was determined she would not let it spoil her moment. She grasped the little lid and gently raised it open. It wasn't a box of golden coins or a chest full of sparkling gems. No, instead it was filled with what appeared to be shackles and rusted chains. Her face fell.

'Manacles! Such Disappointment!' fumed Malaika.

'I did say it was probably a dungeon back in the day,' piped in Perry, who realised he wasn't really adding much to the general atmosphere of despondency.

No one seemed as disheartened as Uncle Hugo, however. His face was almost beetroot with dismay.

'I'm sorry, but did I hear you correctly. Did you claim ownership of that box?' Mr Gentle-Me was questioning Uncle Hugo in his gravelly voice. 'Simply astounding,' he continued. 'Sergeant, you admitted yourself someone had tried to strangle me as I lay helpless in my bed, and I believe I can tell you why?'

'Aye, okay, let's hear it,' growled the Sergeant getting down to proper business. It was, after all, the reason as to why he was dripping wet and in his underwear.

'If you wouldn't mind humouring an old man first, please. Boy, apologies, I've forgotten your name.'

'It's Perry sir.'

'Yes, of course, Perry. Would you mind running up to my room please Perry. I have a small collection of letters...'

Perry waited, unsure if Mr Gentle-Me had finished speaking.

'He will get to the point eventually,' fumed Uncle Hugo.

'... I brought here with me today; they are in my bedside cabinet. Could you please bring them down for me?'

'No problem sir,' said Perry, happy to be involved in a new adventure. He gave Malaika a wink and walked out of the room. He could hear his Uncle Hugo starting to bellow in his wake.

'Sergeant,' he roared, spittle flying from his angry mouth. 'This... this... stop-start timewaster, has been nothing but a nuisance since his arrival in my hotel. I would like you to escort him from the premises. I want him evicted, at once.'

'Steady on Hugo,' said Perry's dad in shock.

'No, I have made my decision. We will send you the bill, but I want you to leave. Now.'

What a disappointment, I thought it was really going to be hidden treasure as well. You would think, in a charming book like this, someone would catch a break and have a happy ending. Ah well, that's real life for you. No, sorry, I cannot let this go, I mean who would put manacles in a box normally reserved for priceless treasure? A very good question. Probably some medieval prankster who is having a good laugh right about now. Maybe a bit peeved it took so long to find it though. Do you keep anything weird in a box? I have a small chest full of my ear and nasal hair at home. Just saying. HB

Chapter 37

Perry, candle extended, started to make his way up the stairs. During the many twists and turns of the jaunt he stumbled across a concerning discovery.

'What's happened over here,' he cried, striding off to investigate. He waved his candle back and forth, his eyes taking in the scene before him. He couldn't help but be worried at the sight of the large hole in the wall that confronted him. A portrait of Pebble Bumbler had also fallen to the floor amongst the discarded bricks and plaster. Perry scratched his head.

'Obviously due the explosion,' he muttered. The cave in downstairs, the ruined kitchen and now this he thought. Despite the setbacks faced today, he was still desperate to save the hotel, but the way things were going there might not even be a hotel standing to save soon. There was nothing he could do for now, so with a sinking heart, he set off for Mr Gentle-Me's room, praying he wouldn't come across any further damage.

On reaching the room, he quickly strode past the unmade bed and bent down next to the bedside drawer. Perry couldn't help but think back to a few hours ago when he thought he had uncovered a dead body. What a day. He opened the drawer to find nothing. Empty! This was almost as dispiriting as the treasure box downstairs.

Was Mr Gentle-Me mistaken? He had been through a lot, perhaps he was a little confused. Perry had a thorough search around the room. He looked under the pillows and beneath the bed, checked the pockets of the jackets hanging in the small wardrobe. Nothing. He looked on top of the wardrobe and under it. Still nothing. Well, almost nothing, he did uncover a spare wig and almost dropped his candle in shock.

Perry admitted defeat, there was nothing here, if it ever had been. Before he left however, impulse drove him to reopen the bedside drawer, one more time. It was then that he noticed it. It was not as empty as he had initially thought. There was something caught in the corner. He gave it a tug and pulled it out, it was a small fragment of purple ribbon. So, there had been something here!

His mind whirring with the implications, Perry headed back downstairs as quickly as he could.

On his return to the drawing room Mr Gentle-Me was crestfallen at the update.

'I guess that settles it in a way. It would seem my suspicions were on the money. Please humour me again Sergeant, I don't need those letters, but I won't lie, they would certainly have helped me with my theory. Perry, can you look again for me please. This time can you look in your uncle's room!'

Everyone gasped and stared at Uncle Hugo. His face looked as if it had been freshly spanked.

'This... this... is **preposterous**,' he shouted. Perry's dad was forced to hold him back, as he tried to get to the elderly Mr Gentle-Me.

'That's not really within my authority,' admitted the Sergeant uncomfortably.

'It's okay Perry,' said his father, who was struggling to contain his brother. 'Go scoot upstairs and have a quick look, I'm sure your uncle has nothing to hide.'

Uncle Hugo looked lost for words at this betrayal, but his bulging eyes told Perry their own story. His uncle had been up to something.

On reaching Uncle Hugo's office, he had a good old rummage around, but he found nothing. Perry had no idea what importance these envelopes had, but if it was going to get Uncle Hugo into trouble, then he just had to find them. Perry's best bet was, of course, the safe. He was sure his uncle had no idea he knew the combination, but it was another dead end. The safe was empty. Perry felt truly defeated. Not finding the envelopes was one thing, but it wasn't lost on him that he had not come across the paperwork for the sale of the hotel either. Was he too late? Had the sale already gone through?

After another quick, but unsuccessful stop, Perry trudged down the stairs, totally deflated. He couldn't bare to see the triumphant look spread all over his uncle's face when he returned empty-handed again.

'Oh, hello Tweezer,' said Perry dejectedly. 'I do apologise, I've ignored you a couple of times today.'

'Hello Perry, how are you?'

Perry was addressing the figure of one Tweezer Bumbler, which sat on a plinth in the hall. He believed he was a big thing back in the day and a picture hanging on the wall wasn't good enough for him. The commissioning of a bronze bust soon followed. Perry, on occasion, would strike up an imaginary conversation with him when bored or lonely.

'I'm not too good I have to admit Tweezer. Ups and downs, and of late... too many downs.'

'Care to elaborate?'

'Stolen letters. It was hoped Uncle Hugo had them, but I couldn't find anything. I'm running out of options now. On the plus side no one is dead and there isn't an enthusiastic strangler roaming the hotel.'

'That's always promising.'

'On the downside, there is a potential amateur strangler on the loose in the hotel.'

'I'll be honest, that's not been the first time.'

'Oh, and Malaika is safe after that explosion.'

'Explosion! So that was the noise,' gushed Tweezer. 'I thought it was that idiot relative of mine Hugolicious attempting to play the tuba again.'

'I'm afraid not, and it looks like the hotel is now falling to pieces. We will be lucky if there is anything left of it after this weekend. Not that it matters, as Uncle Hugo is selling it.'

'That doesn't surprise me, I always thought he was devious.'

'Well, I'm out of ideas, I can't save this place, it's all over. Unless you happen to know where the stolen treasure was hidden?'

'I'm afraid not, I've been stuck in this spot for ages. I barely see anything except for the faces of hot sweaty guests struggling to get their cases up to their rooms. It's no fun I can tell you. Hey, any chance you could get me down in reception or in the drawing room. I was quite important you know; it would be nice to be admired again. I might even be able to help you out.'

'What do you mean?'

'You have a habit of talking when walking, do you know that? Those letters you were looking for, well I have an idea, somewhere you may have forgotten to look.'

'Ah, well if you mean Uncle Hugo's bedroom, I stopped off there as well. It looked like he had been having a party, his furniture was all over the place. Searched it all though, it was as clean as a whistle.'

'That's not where I was thinking of,' teased Tweezer.

'It wasn't?'

'Perry, you are a bright lad. Think about it. Where else could he have hidden them.'

He scratched his head and thought, then thought some more and scratched his head.

'Nope, I'm not getting anything, I have no idea where...'

And then it hit him

'Of course, Tweezer, you are a genius.'

'I know, I know, a beautiful genius who deserves more public attention.'

'Okay, a deal is a deal.'

'Excellent, and any chance that Grubbins can polish me more than once a fortnight?'

'Don't worry Tweezer, consider it done.'

With that Perry rushed down the stairs full of hope. This really would be his last throw of the dice.

I have to hand it to this boy; he does have some imagination. However, if he wants to have a girlfriend at some point in his life, he really needs to stop having these imaginary conversations with inanimate objects. It is just not natural having a conversation when the other party cannot answer you back. Do you not agree? Hello. Are you still there? HB

Chapter 38

Perry crept downstairs and stood outside the drawing room, where another argument seemed to be raging. Sergeant McSweeney and his father were struggling to maintain the peace. They were in the middle, with Uncle Hugo on one side, and the rest of the guests on the other. To Perry, it sounded like he was trying to kick all of them out of the hotel. He had no time for this, however.

His presence was unacknowledged by everyone, except for a wild eyed Malaika, who looked like she wanted to be anywhere but here. He motioned to her to sneak out the room and join him, which she duly did.

'Well, did you find them?' she asked hopefully.

Perry told her his tale of woe.

'So, this is it, is this how it's going to end? Your uncle has gone off the deep end, he's trying to throw everyone out of the hotel.'

'Don't worry, I have a marvellous plan.'

'Oh Perry, I'm not sure I can take anymore of your plans.'

'We need to search his walk-in wardrobe.'

'Are you insane, that would take weeks!'

'Under normal circumstances I would agree, but thankfully I have that marvellous plan, didn't I mention it? Just make sure your little disciple follows us upstairs, it will be all hands to the pump. Trust me.' He guided her up the stairs with Pretzel in tow.

'I hate to burst your bubble Perry, but it's widely known that you have a very inflated opinion of your plans.'

'Listen, you are talking to the boy who once scored 180 by only throwing one dart!'

'Big deal, I once had a strike at ten pin bowling, and I was only using a ping pong ball!'

'Oh really, you want to do this do you,' snapped Perry as they continued to climb.

'What happened here?' gasped Malaika when she saw the damage to the wall.

'Oh that, its old news, the hotel is crumbling down around us. Anyway, the bowling, mildly stirring, but not as impressive as the time I completed the crossword in the Little Didwob Gazette... without even looking at the clues.'

'If that's the case then you could not have failed to notice the front page of said paper. Its celebration of the winning goal I scored for Little Didwob United in the cup. It was a beautiful free kick, bending like a banana, right into the top corner. I did that with a ping pong ball as well after the regular football went flat.'

'Ha, very good, I didn't want to have to tell you this, but I wrote that #1 hit song for that silly band you like, Balooga Razzamatazz.'

'You leave them out of this,' Malaika warned.

'Yes - The Whole of My Hole - it was all about my favourite pair of underwear. We had been through thick, and so much thin, together over the years, but they were so threadbare and fragile at the end. Needless to say, the inevitable happened. Sad days. I want you to remember that heavenly gusset the next time you listen to that little ditty. The words take on a completely new meaning when you know the inspiration behind them.'

'Lies, lies...! Well, I was once out having a late walk in the forest and before I knew it, I was surrounded by a pack of rabid slavering wolves. Actually, the more I think of it they may have been werewolves. I'm sure one of them had a lazy eye which reminded me of that lady, you know, the one who works in the post office. Anyway, there I was, surrounded, with nothing to protect me but a ping pong ball...'

'Okay, enough, I'm calling absolute nonsense on that one. And what's your fixation with ping pong balls anyway? When you are making up stories other sporting equipment is available. **OUCH.**'

Something smacked Perry in the forehead. Something fast, white, round and painful. Something like a ...

Malaika caught the white blur that rebounded back towards her. She held it aloft between her fingers. 'For the record it's my lucky ping pong ball and I carry it everywhere with me. Do you have a problem with that?'

'Nooooo,' muttered Perry sheepishly who was still rubbing the stinging spot above his eyebrows.

'Oh look, we are here.'

Indeed, they were, Uncle Hugo's warehouse of a wardrobe lay ahead of them.

'Okay, time for you to unravel your amazing plan,' said Malaika.

They entered the room, which could not have looked more different from when they were last both visitors.

'My plan is simplicity itself,' said Perry as he ruffled about in his trouser pocket. 'Give this to Pretzel to sniff, then ask him to find the rest of it.'

Perry handed her the small piece of purple ribbon he had found earlier.

'You are joking? He's not that kind of dog.'

'Of course he is, they can all do it. Amazing sense of smell they have.'

'Listen, this little munchkin just looks lovely and poops a lot. A great deal if truth be told. You've seen the size of them. Imagine sniffing those monsters afterwards! His little nose must be broken beyond repair.'

'Well, let's try it shall we. In case you hadn't noticed, we are considerably desperate.'

Malaika called to Pretzel who was at her side in seconds, tail wagging frantically. She let him smell the ribbon then gave him his instructions.

'Off you go Pretzel.

Off you go.

Go get it.

Find it.

Sniff it out.

Pretzel, please move.'

He just sat there looking at her, panting gently.

'What were you saying about your grand plan?'

'A famous actor once gave me some advice,' said Perry, who was still rubbing his forehead. 'Never work with children and animals...'

'Why you....'

Suddenly, Pretzel dashed off between the endless rails of clothes.

'Quick, follow that dog,' Perry cried.

It darted left... it sprinted right... it scurried up... it raced down... it scrambled around in a circle... it fled in and out of sight and finally it skidded to a halt.

Perry and Malaika did their best to follow Pretzel in the darkened maze, to the point where they were both quite lost and out of breath.

'Look, he's stopped,' said Perry.

'Next to a potato sack?'

'No, that's not a potato sack, that is a monk's habit.'

'Why would your uncle own a...'

'As a joke. To my dad, when he developed his.... bald spot. That's how my uncle works. But it can't be this. It doesn't have any pockets. There's nowhere it could be hidden...'

Perry closed his mouth with a large click of his teeth.

'What was that? Are you okay?'

'Look,' he said holding his candle aloft. 'There, in the hood.'

Perry lifted out a pile of yellowed envelopes tied together with purple ribbon. They both looked at each other.

'Well, well, well, just what has your uncle been up to?'

'Mr Gentle-Me was right,' Perry whispered.

Perry placed the recovered envelopes inside his jacket and with Pretzels' help, they exited the room as fast as their flickering candle allowed.

When they both made their way downstairs, it seemed their absence had not been noticed, and the same argument was still raging on.

'I insist you get out of this hotel,' hollered Uncle Hugo like a stuck needle in a record.

Perry strode in and finally the room fell into silence.

Uncle Hugo's round face slit into an evil smirk when he noticed the empty-handed Perry.

'As expected, as I told you,' he spat. 'You come into **MY** hotel and accuse **ME** of theft! **YOU** are the thieves,' he ranted. 'You have stolen my **TIME**. You have pilfered my **HOSPITALITY**. You have pinched my **GENEROSITY**. I want you out. **OUT**.'

Mr Gentle-Me looked at Perry with sad eyes, his skin looked greyer than previously.

'Thanks for looking Perry, I'm sorry if it was a wild goose chase, I appreciate your time and effort,' he wheezed.

'No problem at all,' replied a now beaming Perry, who made a point of staring at his uncle. He reached into his jacket and pulled out the envelopes. 'I believe these are yours Mr Gentle-Me.'

The silence in the room could be cut with a knife. Perry could not help but notice the uneasy frantic look now plastered on his uncle's face.

'What's that you have there? I've never seen those before. Look Sergeant, I have a hotel to run, and I would very much like you to assist me in removing these individuals from the premises. I will not have any trouble in my hotel.' Uncle Hugo was almost pleading now, he was rubbing his sweaty hands together.

'This collection of letters,' whispered Mr Gentle-Me who ignored Uncle Hugo and was now addressing the room, 'will help to prove whom my attacker was. The terrible act he was prepared to carry out due to sheer greed. An evil individual. A con artist and a rogue. Everyone, the person who tried to strangle me in my room was none other than... Erstwhile Bumbler!'

The room took a collective gasp. Perry felt his legs turn to rubber at the shocking revelation. How could Mr Gentle-Me betray him like this.

'The man is an old fool,' blustered Uncle Hugo. 'He does not know what he is talking about, I was nowhere near him, those letters were obviously planted. I have said this already, but he is a sandwich short of a picnic. He is befuddled and confused. Probably a bed wetter as well. I really should check that. Perry, take a note for later, we will add the extra cost of mattress cleaning to his bill.'

Slowly, Uncle Hugo's addled brain absorbed what Mr Gentle-Me had just said.

'Hang on... Erstwhile?' He turned to his brother, 'Oh how could you? I'm so disappointed. Attacking an old man, a poor bed wetter! Sergeant, take this disgusting criminal away. And his son for good measure, he was probably in on it as well. The apple, as they say, does not fall far from the tree. And that girl too, I always thought she looked rather shifty, look at all the damage she has caused tonight. Arrest the three of them.'

He crossed his arms across his expansive chest, head held high in what he surely felt was a triumphant pose.

Again, the room gasped.

'Gee whiz.'

'I... I had my suspicions you know; nobody can be that nice.'

The Sergeant was starting to develop a slight twitch.

Grubbins gave a sob and fled out of the room.

'Yes,' continued Mr Gentle-Me, doing his best to ignore the antics of his audience. 'Erstwhile Bumbler tried to kill me in order to keep his terrible secret...'

'A... A secret?' repeated Sorry Noakes, eyes wide. It was obvious his normally plain, bland, and placid days as a purveyor of socks had never prepared him for quite a night such as this.

'Indeed, a dark one at that.'

Perry's dad stood there in disbelief.

'Look, you have this all wrong, I am not a murderer, even a failed one.'

Despite his pleas of innocence, everyone in the room was slowly edging away from him. Everyone that was bar the Sergeant.

Perry was numb. All his dreams and plans for the hotel, for his family, it had all collapsed around him. Everything was ruined. Tears began prickling at his eyes.

'Dad... what's happening?'

The Sergeant, still swathed in damp towels, large stomach protruding, stood next to Perry's father, ready for the arrest.

However, Mr Gentle-Me wasn't finished.

'No Sergeant, that's not Erstwhile Bumbler,' he said. He turned towards Uncle Hugo and gave him a sly wink. 'And I can prove it.'

Mistaken identity. The worst kind of identity. I shall admit, when it comes to fashion, I have a certain style, it works for me, so I wear it, always. Unfortunately, whenever I visited Berlin during the cold war, everyone would mistake me for a spy. Both sides. Just popping out for some lunch time bratwurst, usually entailed having to avoid a kidnapping and at least two assassination attempts. Lying like this on the beach in Ibiza may draw some funny looks, I may be mistaken for a loon, but I will take that everyday of the week. HB

Chapter 39

'Look over there, at the window, it's the **STRANGLER...**' screamed Uncle Hugo.

Everyone turned in the direction of his trembling finger and stared.

Seizing the opportunity, he made a break for it, but not before shoving Sergeant McSweeney, who quickly became entangled in his towels, falling in a wriggling thud to the floor. Uncle Hugo leapt over him and sprinted towards the exit in a bid for freedom.

Everyone was disappointed that there was no grotesque face pressed up against the rain lashed window and they all turned to witness the escape.

Uncle Hugo was not a fit individual, and it took an inordinate amount of time for him to shuffle out of the drawing room. Jimmy James Jr. even had time to scrutinise his watch, such was the speed of the hotelier.

Eventually, as if in slow motion, the sweating red-faced fugitive finally exited from view.

'He finally made it, I was of a mind to offer him a push,' Jimmy James Jr. commented.

Then, from reception, came a chorus of calamity.

SCHHLOOOOOP...

OOOOOOOOOH...

CRASH...

OOOOOOOOFFFF...

CLUNK-CLUNK...

CLATTER...

OOOOOOOOFFFF...

CLUNK-CLUNK...

TINKLE...

BARK...

For those in the drawing room, not privy to the magical mayhem playing out only a few feet from them, it was an intoxicating mix of screeching, wailing, and smashing. For Grubbins, who was currently passing the reception desk, it was a never to be seen again clip of cringeworthy chaos and confusion.

That pesky dog. He had recognised it now. Especially after the enormous poo it had just brazenly deposited on his lovely, polished floor. He had just returned with his cleaning equipment to dispose of the offending article, when it happened.

He saw M'lud running out of the drawing room as if the very devil himself was chasing him, which to be fair wasn't very fast. Grubbins however still did not have time to shout a warning.

An expensive loafer sunk into the squidgy foul-smelling mass and Hugo found himself accelerating across the reception. All pretence of control was abandoned. He was sliding and gliding in the most undignified way, his arms wheeling in circles, his face a collage of fear, disgust, and horror as he whimpered.

There was an almighty clatter and clash that put the kitchen explosion to shame. The slippery slide of shame had come to an eventual end due to a collision with the suit of armour once belonging to Violet-Palava Bumbler.

Then the screaming began.

'What now?' said Perry's dad who had bent over to help the flailing Sergeant back on to his feet. The almost unbelievable revelations by Mr Gentle-Me were still ringing in his ears and there was no room for more competition.

He was still the first to venture out into reception to survey the scene. There was a smell, lingering in the air, of things best not talked about.

'Bring that mop would you Grubbins,' he cried.

Carefully minding where he stood, as did the others who followed him, they made their way out of the drawing room.

'HELP ME

HELP ME

PLEASE, IT'S A GHOST. IT'S COME FOR ME. I KNEW IT WOULD. IT FINALLY HAS ME...'

Uncle Hugo was lying, whimpering on the floor, the recent events of the night had taken their toll, he looked broken, he had finally cracked. To be fair there was a heavy looking suit of armour lying on top of him which wasn't helping matters.

'A GHOST. A GHOST. CAN YOU SEE IT. IT KNOWS WHAT I HAVE DONE. IT'S BEEN WATCHING ME FOR YEARS. IT'S JUDGEMENT DAY...'

'I... I see it too...,' jumped Sorry Noakes, emitting another high-pitched whistling scream, before collapsing to the floor in yet another faint.

'Gee whiz so do I,' muttered a horrified Jimmy James Jr. who pulled a length of his hair across his eyes as a temporary blindfold.

For it was not an empty suit of armour that was slowly crushing the life out of the hysterical Uncle Hugo, its helmet had been displaced as had other sections of the suit. There was a bald pale ghostly face that peered down at him from inside the armour, another deathly white limb could be seen flopping around. The phantom was uttering demonic curses from its white lips as it moaned and groaned.

Uncle Hugo tried his best to squirm out from underneath his hellish captor. His eyes were bloodshot and bulging in horror, his once carefully parted hair was now a wild mess, at least three of the buttons on his jacket had fired off into the night. He reached out a pleading arm towards Sergeant McSweeney.

'Please, please, arrest me,' he croaked. 'Get me out of this paranormal prison and into a real one. I beg you; I beg you. Please, take me, take me away before IT drags me down into a fiery pit...'

Sergeant McSweeney was at a complete loss. He didn't know what to do, he was too busy trying to make sense of what was playing out before him. His training had not prepared him to deal with ghosts, ghouls, and goblins. On the plus side, it wasn't a headless horseman, but it was still a grim sight. He could hear a faint groan escape from the spectre that lay across the blubbering Bumbler.

'Well... I... Never...,' came a voice from behind them. It was Malaika who was doing her best to see from behind the throng of onlookers. 'Let me through,' she commanded as she forced her way to the front, all sharp elbows.

She strode over to the ghostly apparition and bent over to look at it more closely. She squinted and stared, gaped, and leered. Obviously satisfied with what she saw a little dance suddenly broke out, followed by her repeatedly punching the air in what appeared to be jubilation.

'That... That Hugo fellow is not the only one going around the bend, I hope it's not catching,' said Sorry who had recovered from his light-headedness.

'What is happening out here,' gasped Mr Gentle-Me who had finally made it out to reception on shaky legs, his thin hands tightly clutching his precious letters close to him.

'I... am making a citizen's arrest,' proclaimed Malaika to everyone in the hotel.

'Can she do that?' Jimmy James Jr. asked the Sergeant.

The Sergeant had a bemused look upon his face, the day had also taken its toll on him.

'Well, I'm not stopping her, let's just see what happens, hopefully someone will explain.'

Malaika reached into the ancient wooden box she was carrying and began to pull out the rusty chains and manacles within. She carefully snapped one on to the exposed white wrist of the wraith and another on to the ankle of Uncle Hugo, who was still pinned underneath and was beginning to drool quite excessively.

'Can she do that?' Jimmy James Jr. asked the Sergeant.

'Well, I don't have any handcuffs,' he barked back. He realised however it was time to take control of matters.

'Okay, okay, what exactly are ye doing here?' he said to Malaika.

'I have just, among other things, made a citizen's arrest,' she boasted proudly, there was a fire burning brightly in her eyes. 'Yes, a citizen's arrest, as it is quite clear that Hugo Bumbler here is a villain, an unsavoury character, a...'

She looked over at Mr Gentle-Me.

'A con man,' he puffed.

'Yes,' continued Malaika, 'a fraudster, who tried to take Mr Gentle-Me's life and his collection of prized envelopes.'

'Hear, hear,' rasped Mr Gentle-Me who shook them in the air.

'Aye, well we can get to the bottom of that down at the station,' said the Sergeant. 'But what's this we have here,' he gestured towards the gruesome monster, half in half out of the suit of armour.

'Hang on, isn't that Ms Harrumph,' said Perry, coming closer to the prone figure, while deftly stepping over the large brown skid mark that marred the floor. 'What's happened to her? Where is her hair? Has she had a flour bath?'

'This is not Ms Harrumph, or whatever she is calling herself,' said Malaika coolly as she stood over her. 'This is none other than Sabrina Marx...'

'Away! The weatherwoman from the radio!' blurted out the Sergeant, who scratched his white close-cropped hair in disbelief.

'No... No, that wasn't her name. It's her from that smutty TV game show, on THAT channel. The one where they all swap each others' clothes. Disgusting stuff. I only watch in order to compose comprehensive complaint letters,' claimed Sorry Noakes.

'I don't think we have anyone in my country with a name like that,' added Jimmy James Jr. so as not to be left out.

'Perry, educate them,' sighed Malaika.

Everyone turned to Perry for the answer, but all he could supply in return was a meek shrug of his shoulders and an apologetic face.

'Oh okay,' said Malaika exasperated, 'I'm glad you paid attention to that little briefing I gave you earlier. Everyone, to all of you this is Ms Harrumph, a fellow guest of the hotel. To everyone outside of this hotel however, she is none other than Sabrina Marx, daughter of one Sinclair Marx, also known as... the Plimsoll Bandit.'

'Of course,' said Perry.

'Better late than never,' said Malaika. 'It would seem she has been playing a little game with you all since her arrival. If she was here claiming to be a salesperson, I can assure you she is not, regardless of what she may have told you.

'You mean, you can't buy Chudge?' queried Perry's dad disappointedly.

'She is here to reclaim her father's stolen goods.'

Malaika turned on her flashlight and shone it on the prone figures and around the floor. It was now glittering with gems and precious golden artifacts. There, spilling out of a discarded piece of armour, was a glittering thick silver chain embedded with a series of sapphires.

'Everyone, I give you the Krustovia Crown Jewels!'

'Amazing, so it WAS all true, they were here under our noses the whole time,' said Perry's dad.

'Indeed,' grinned Malaika, 'I never doubted it for a second.'

'**Looky. . . Looky. . . Looky. . .**

Treasure. . . Lovely treasure. . . I have first dibs on that shiny crown thing. . . I have always wanted a hat. . .'

'But why does she look like a bald ghost?' asked Perry's father, doing his best to ignore the disembodied voice behind him.

'It's plaster,' cut in Perry, 'she is covered in plaster and dust. We found a hole in the wall upstairs; it must have been her. She dug out the wall to get to the stolen exhibit pieces, while you were all dealing with the explosion in the kitchen.'

'Which she must have arranged.' Perry's father was finally beginning to understand just what had been happening in the hotel.

'Sabrina Marx also suffers from the same condition as her father and she is completely bald,' added Malaika. 'I'll be honest, I didn't even realise when I arrived earlier.'

'It was a very impressive wig, considering the issues we had earlier with the wind,' said Perry.

'Indeed, I really must find out where she purchased it,' rasped Mr Gentle-Me.

'But why was she hiding in the suit of armour?' asked Perry's dad.

'I'm assuming this wasn't part of her original plan,' surmised Malaika. 'She certainly wouldn't have been expecting both the Sergeant and myself to have shown up tonight. She may have worried that one of us would recognise her for who she really was, even with a disguise. Or, as she thought there was a murderer in the hotel, the armour would provide her with a measure of safety. Regardless, it was an excellent hiding place, she was able to walk around the hotel and no one gave this dented old thing a second thought. And, when the coast was clear, she could easily sneak out of the hotel.'

There was a groaning from the floor as Sabrina Marx began to come around.

I'VE BEEN HIT, HIT BY A CAR,' she moaned, then suddenly realised she was surrounded by everyone and chained to a shivering, crying Uncle Hugo.

'WHAAAT!' she snarled, realising the game was up.

I find myself lost for words! Except to say that if it had indeed been something paranormal inhabiting that suit of armour, then I would have brought in my good friend Bobbin Beanfast. Do not worry, you do not need to know about him until a later book! HB

Chapter 40

'You know what this means partner,' said a beaming Malaika to Perry.

'We did it. I still don't know how, but we did it. Now we can save the hotel after all!' They both gave each other an enthusiastic high five, much to the bemusement of the others.

'What do you mean, save the hotel? Save it from what exactly?' asked Perry's dad.

Perry realised his mistake with his father in earshot, he felt he had no option now but to confess.

'I'm sorry dad, I found out a little while ago, but I didn't know how to tell you. I'll admit at first, I didn't know if I wanted to. With you and mum not speaking, if we were to leave the hotel then at least you would get back together.'

Tears were starting to well up in Perry's eyes.

'Son, it's okay, we will be fine, all of us,' he rested his hand on Perry's shoulder. 'Now, what are the pair of you up to?'

'It's Uncle Hugo... he is planning on selling the hotel. I saw it with my own eyes. I read the letter. Some organisation called Quantum Affiliation, they offered to buy the land and Uncle Hugo was more than happy to sell it to them. But it's okay now dad. We did it. We did the impossible. We found the stolen treasure. Half that reward money will be ours, and we can use it, use it to help us buy the hotel. For us, to keep it in the family. You and mum can run it the way you want to. All those great ideas you have, the ones Uncle Hugo never listens to. With you in charge, and Uncle Hugo gone, mum will come back. All three of us can run the High Hill Hotel together, as a family.'

Perry ran over and embraced his dazed looking father, who gave him a bear like hug in return.

'Sell the hotel,' he muttered to himself in disbelief.

Perry's father turned to look at his brother, who was still sitting, quivering on the ground. He looked quite deranged, his hair in disarray, black shadows around his eyes, and he was twitching nervously. His velvet tuxedo was ruined, and one eyebrow was perched on his face higher than the other, giving him a sad comical appearance. It was unclear if he was now even capable of a proper conversation.

'Hugolicious, is this true? Our home. Our family business. We Bumblers have run this hotel for an eternity. Were you really going to sell it?'

His voice was getting louder and shriller with every word, until he was almost shouting, his face as dark as the thunder outside. In all his days Perry had never seen his father so cross.

Perry looked down at his uncle, a shell of his former self. If he was to take a leaf out of Jimmy James Jr's book, then he would have rated his uncle's aura as 'deflated balloon'.

Uncle Hugo stopped his swaying and looked up at his brother. He wiped away some snot with the back of his hand and began to laugh manically.

'You are too late,' he giggled. 'It's as good as sold now, the contract has been signed and delivered. By the end of the week this horrid place will be as good as closed.' He laughed again his eyes were wild and void of sanity, he seemed to have lost his faculties.

'Sold...,' said Perry, his stomach sinking.

'Too late...,' sighed Malaika.

'Closed...,' repeated Perry's father in disbelief.

'Yes, **SOLD**,' roared Uncle Hugo with great delight, 'and I can't wait until they tear this miserable place down.'

A sting in the tale, I knew it. Not only sold, but to be knocked down! Torn down. Destroyed. Levelled. Flattened. Violently Deconstructed. A great pity. I wonder if they are planning on building a golf course. I do find myself in between memberships at the moment. I find some players can be very precious about bad language and having to dodge vigorously thrown clubs. HB

Chapter 41

Uncle Hugo rattled the chain connected to his ankle. 'Sergeant, can you please have this removed immediately. I have been illegally detained. It would seem the real criminal is lying over there, dressed like a medieval ghost.'

Uncle Hugo was trying to pull himself together again. His little 'episode' coming to an end. You could almost hear the cogs whirring in his head as he tried to extract himself from the situation. He patted his hair down and tried to adjust the mess that was his attire.

Ms Harrumph/Sabrina Marx gave another moan.

'I would also like to converse with my lawyer, there has been a terrible miscarriage of justice performed tonight. I'll be suing the lot of you for defamation. NOW Sergeant,' he hissed menacingly holding up his shackle. 'I'll also need to speak to my business contacts and update them on the damage caused here tonight, although it shouldn't bother them too much, you have probably saved them some work.'

Despite the chain around his ankle, he stood up and began to look around reception.

'I won't miss this place one little bit. I have stomached as much as I can. It confined me, stifled me. Having to be polite to fools and idiots like you lot all day, it's so incredibly draining, so tedious.' Uncle Hugo began pulling faces at everyone.

He's really not well thought Perry to himself.

'I will arrange for my belongings to be collected and then I will begin my travels. My brother Erstwhile, your foolish son Perry, I wish you both the best of luck in whatever mediocre endeavour you next seek to pursue. Trust me, our paths will not cross again,' he grinned savagely.

'I don't think so,' came the hoarse voice of Mr Gentle-Me, who's own face was getting as red as his neck. 'Sergeant do not remove the restraints from this man. As I claimed earlier, he is a fraud. You both have nothing to worry about. I have been a businessman for many, many years and I know my way around a legal deal or two. Perhaps what you have said is true. Maybe contracts have been signed and issued, the i's dotted and the t's crossed, the discussions concluded. But I do know one thing, there is not a court in the land that will uphold this sale.'

Mr Gentle-Me shuffled over and stood in front of Uncle Hugo and stared. Uncle Hugo however averted his eyes and looked down at the floor as if a naughty schoolboy.

'The fact of the matter, is that only the owner of something can legally sell it, and this hotel is no different.'

'But he does own it,' said Perry. 'The hotel is always passed down through the family, to the oldest child, that's been the way for centuries. With Uncle Hugo not having any children

I guess he would rather sell it now rather than pass it over to us at some point.'

'My son is correct. He legally owns this place lock, stock and barrel and if he has sold it there is nothing we can do. It's over.'

'No,' commanded Mr Gentle-Me, 'far from it, the owner of this hotel has not sold it. In fact, from what I have seen, the owner of this hotel has not been calling the shots at all.'

'I really don't understand. What are you trying to say?' said Perry's dad.

'What I am trying to say Mr Bumbler, and I do apologise for not having been more direct, is that **YOU** are the rightful owner of the High Hill Hotel!'

'Don't be silly, it's my deranged, traitorous, chained up brother here that owns the hotel. Or at least he used to.'

'Well, I have evidence to the contrary,' said Mr Gentle-Me, holding aloft his pile of recovered letters. 'I'm not sure how to break this to you, but the fact of the matter is you are Hugo Bumbler and that insane criminal standing over there is your younger brother, Erstwhile. Somehow, at some point, you have both switched places!'

Well, I will be a monkey's uncle. What type of switcheroo shenanigans is that all about? Luckily for you it is all revealed on the next page. But wait a second. Soak in the tension. Bathe in the suspense. Anticipation is everything you know. It takes a while to write a book, you can at least read it slowly and savour it........... Okay, you may go now. HB

Chapter 42

The Sergeant cut off the gasps of surprise and shock by stepping into the centre of the room and holding up his hand. The audience fell into silence, no one daring to intervene. He stood there thinking to himself for what seemed liked minutes, but it could only have been seconds. He was oddly aware of the fact he was still dripping.

A series of wild thoughts were racing through his head. This place was a circus. A madhouse. Tonight, had covered murder, thievery, explosions, the walking dead, ghosts, rescues, and abnormal dog poo. And those were just some of the things he knew about. He was not going to pretend he fully understood what had happened here. But he did know one thing, the longer he remained, the more likely something else was going to happen in this cursed hotel.

'Okay everybody, there is only one course o' action. Until backup arrives, I'm placing every single one o' ye... under arrest.'

The room erupted into a frenzy, a cacophony of raised voices with everyone gesturing wildly at the injustice of it all. The sergeant immediately regretted his decision.

'Sergeant, Sergeant,' cooed Mr Gentle-Me who was suddenly full of life and vigour as the salesman did what he did best, brokered a deal.

'I appreciate what has been discussed here sounds like madness, I almost didn't believe it myself, up until the point where I was strangled that is. Please believe me, the two people currently incapacitated are the only ones you need to be concerned about. Let me offer a suitable compromise. Should anyone act out of turn for the remainder of our stay then you can happily arrest them. Tomorrow, when help arrives, we will all gladly queue up to answer your questions and give our statements.'

Having realised his fictional hero - Inspector Budgerigar of the Yard - would never have made this type of overstep, the Sergeant made a show of considering the suggestion and then gave a gruff nod of his head in agreement. Everyone gave a sigh of relief.

'Excellent, and I would very much like for you to hold on to these letters of mine. They are key evidence, and you will find them very enlightening. Especially the letter confirming the birthmark on the bottom of the youngest child - Erstwhile. A birthmark I witnessed when he was born, 40 or so years ago in this very hotel and unfortunately, very recently in that unsavoury display in the drawing room earlier.'

Then, on cue, both Grubbins and Belinda appeared, carrying trays laden with sandwiches and cakes.

'Careful everyone,' whispered Perry's father, 'best we don't let this spoil a happy ending,' he smiled.

Something caught the eye of Perry. It was vague and foggy, there but not there, a slight shimmer like gossamer. He looked harder, concentrated, the dim light making it increasingly harder. Perry froze. No. It couldn't be. But it was. Wasn't it? The old man from his dream. Standing there on the reception steps. He held up a hand as if in gratitude. A smile swept his face then he was gone. Vanishing into the gloom. Perry's heart was racing.

'Are you okay Perry,' said a beaming Malaika. 'You look like you have seen a ghost.'

'I... I'm not sure, maybe I just did,' and he grinned at her.

Everyone stayed within the vicinity of reception and the drawing room, as the night slowly passed, and the wind and rain began to lessen.

It was around 5am when the Sergeant's men arrived at the hotel door, and they were all glad to lay eyes on each other. They also had the opportunity to compliment him on the clown costume he was wearing. It had been retrieved for him from Hugo's extensive wardrobe after he had finally dried off. Unfortunately, there wasn't much that would fit him, according to the young lad Perry, but he was just relieved to be able to cover up his boxer shorts and string vest. Now, when thinking about it, he was sure he had just been made the butt of a joke.

Both the fake Uncle Hugo and false Ms Harrumph were taken into custody, and as agreed the witness statements freely flowed. The extensive investigation blossomed, the press soon became involved and as the distraught Sergeant predicted, the paperwork was simply insurmountable...

Paperwork! As a well renowned author of some standing, I know my way around paperwork, and it is not enjoyable. It rises and rises and rarely lowers itself – unless a paper avalanche counts. It is messy and due to my phobia over staples, it gets disjointed and lost. Let us not dwell on papercuts either. Hallelujah Bumbler may be gone, but he will not be forgotten. His artistic genius taken from us all too soon, due to the deadly nature of paperwork. We should also shed a tear for the poor Sergeant too, for he deserves it. HB

Chapter 43

One short week later found both Perry and Malaika sitting on a rustic wooden bench on the leaf strewn grounds of the High Hill Hotel. The riotous storm was nothing more than a distant memory and things were returning to normal, if that word could even be used again.

A temporary bridge had successfully been erected, meaning there was no more need for the arduous rowing of boats back and forth across the river to the village. With a bridge in place, it also meant that repair work to the hotel was well underway.

'I have to say, this is a fantastic picture,' gushed Perry as he looked at the front page of the Gazette. In the photo, Malaika was beaming proudly. In both her hands, held high over her head, was an enormous cheque. Its oversized proportions made Malaika look tiny. It was her well earned reward for recovering the Krustovia crown jewels. The giant offering had been presented to her by none other than the Prime Minister, who grinned inanely in the photo.

But that was not all, for pinned to her chest was a rather ostentatious medal, another reward for recovering the long-lost stolen treasure. This had been presented to her by the delighted Krustovia ambassador, who was also squeezed into the photo.

The paper was also full of stories about the improving diplomatic relations between the two countries, their decades long frosty association, now beginning to thaw.

'It's a rather nifty looking medal,' Perry continued as he folded the paper. He stared at the golden star, 'I'm glad you found a good use for it.'

'I did indeed.' Malaika scratched behind the ear of Pretzel who was sitting patiently at her feet. The medal now took pride of place around his neck, hanging from his first ever collar. There were not many dog tags out there as special as this one, and he seemed very pleased with himself as if he realised it.

'I might need some grooming tips from you Perry, I can't seem to do much with his hair, it's sticking out all over the place, you'd think he had been chewing power cables.'

Perry laughed and attempted to run his fingers through his own hair, but they got stuck halfway through. Time to change the subject.

'It was very generous of you to adopt him, if not it wouldn't have been long before the villagers chased him off with pitchforks and flaming torches.'

'And how could I not adopt him, especially after all he did. Finding me in the wall and making that bad man fall into the armour. Yes, you did, you did.' She ruffled the wiry hair on Pretzel's head and produced a treat from nowhere, which he gobbled down quickly.

'After all that there was no way my Mum could say no. Of course, he's going to cost me a small fortune in historical poo fines, but that's a small price to pay to have his record cleared.'

Perry laughed. 'Well, you can certainly afford it.'

'And one day in the future, while you are still running this grand hotel with your mum and dad, I will be going off to university... to become an archaeologist.'

'Wow, for real?'

'For real,' they gave each other a fist bump.

'Can I ask what happened with the cheque. Did you have to take it to a bank?'

'Oh, that's just for the photos. They transferred the money straight into my mum's bank account. They let me keep it though, I have it stuck up on my bedroom wall.'

Perry smiled; she deserved it. The money would go a long way to fulfil her studies and it had already helped set up her mother's new computer repair business.

'What about you Perry? Not having second thoughts about giving me all the reward money, I hope? I mean, I know you just got your own hotel but let's be honest, it's been a little banged up over the last few days.'

'Don't you worry about the repairs, that's all been taken care of. After all the publicity, we had a theatre company approach us. We sold off all of Uncle Hugo's walk-in wardrobe for a very tidy sum. They were boasting when they left that there is not a show in the land they can't perform now.'

'Oh, that's fantastic news, I'll be sad to see it go though, that was great fun dressing up in there.'

'Which reminds me, I did save this for you,' Perry reached under the bench and pulled out a carefully hidden cardboard box which he presented to her.

Malaika slowly opened it, and her eyes sprang wide.

'Oh Perry, thank you.' She held up the shimmering golden ballgown that lay within. 'I love this, and it will really go with Pretzel's medal. I can't wait for us both to strut our stuff around Little Didwob.'

Perry laughed.

'Of course, I'm hoping you will join us,' and she gave him a quick peck on the cheek.

A cheek that instantly turned scarlet, such was the force of Perry's blushing.

Pretzel gave a gruff little bark as if he was also in agreement.

The three of them sat, enjoying the morning, while basking in the heat of Perry's face.

That was heartwarming was it not. I will just admit it, I am a big softy at the end of the day. Now if you excuse me, I think I have something in my eye as it is beginning to tear up. HB

Chapter 44

'So, should we do this then?' asked Malaika.

'Sure, why not, an actual theory of yours resolved itself. We both know this will never happen again, so let's make the most of it.'

Malaika grinned and from her rucksack eagerly pulled out her tin foil covered book of the bizarre and strange. She opened it to the correct page, twirled her pen and began.

'As we both now know, Mr Gentle-Me was correct in every way. His letters pretty much confirmed that your uncle was a complete fraud. The police verified the handwriting, and it was your grandmothers. Erstwhile Bumbler was the younger twin with the birthmark on the bottom, which was mentioned in the correspondence. The police also tracked down a retired nurse from a couple of villages over, who still remembered the twins, even after all these years. I guess it helps to have unusual names after all. To think, if your uncle hadn't worn a kilt that day, we would never have known. Sorry, to be more specific, if your uncle had worn underpants that day like a normal person, we would never have known.

The letters also tell of a cricket injury your father once had, took a bit of a whack to the head apparently.'

'Yes, my dad's old scar. I questioned him about that, he vaguely remembers some of it. He recalls being hit on the head and being knocked out. The headaches and the two full weeks off school he enjoyed. His only other recollection was that he was now sleeping in the bottom bunk bed rather than the top one. Oh, that and his dislike of pickled herring, which his mother insisted he usually loved. Honestly, how ridiculous is that. I can't believe he just allowed someone to steal his whole identity.'

'Don't be too hard on him Perry, this is your evil toad of an uncle we are talking about. Can you imagine what it must have been like growing up with him as a brother? Lying, conspiring, scheming. It's small wonder your dad didn't end up insane, or worse. I very much doubt it was an accident either, his younger brother probably planned everything. Maybe that's why your dad just accepted it all. I mean, their own mother didn't even realise. Your uncle knew the hotel would never be his, so he decided to take matters into his own hands.'

Malaika stopped and made some updates in her book. She flicked a couple of pages ahead, made another note and then began again.

'I remember you telling me once, that even though you never knew your grandmother, you were glad you didn't. Your dad said she was cold and distant, despite what Mr Gentle-Me wants to remember. She was more interested in running the hotel, and as long as there was someone to carry on the family tradition, that was all she was interested in. Don't be mad at him Perry. They looked identical in every way, but while your dad was kind-hearted, your uncle was sneaky and devious. He knew exactly what he needed to do to keep up the pretence. Listen to the music your dad liked, read the correct books, eat the right foods. He just started changing things back again, little by little, over time. So long as he kept his birthmark hidden, he had nothing to worry about.'

Perry laughed. 'Did you know that during my uncle's first night in jail he plucked out every single hair of his moustache. In the morning, he tried to tell everyone there had been a terrible mistake - they had arrested the wrong brother! His ridiculous haircut and pot belly notwithstanding, they wisely chose to ignore him. Got to love a trier though. Thankfully he eventually admitted everything, and we can all move on now.

He knew straight away that Mr Gentle-Me had recognised his birthmark. He had stopped hiding it with makeup years ago. It was the old letters though, he was scared there was something that could incriminate him, that provided the proof to the ramblings of an old man. He snuck into the room to steal them after lunch. He claims Mr Gentle-Me was waking up and was about to catch him red handed, so he panicked and strangled him. Or so he thought.'

'Good old Mr Gentle-Me, he was the real hero of this whole unsavoury episode,' said Malaika.

'Indeed, we owe him so much. The lawyers he put us in touch with have been working very hard. Not only is the hotel firmly under the ownership of my dad but the company, who thought they had bought it, have been informed the deal is null and void. We even got a letter from one of their executives, a Genghis Stomp, with an improved offer, but we turned it down. They were not happy, but there is nothing they can do about it. Anyway, enough about this place, what did you find out about the stolen treasure?'

'Well, despite being in prison, the Plimsoll Bandit made it his business to know your uncle's business. As soon as he caught wind that your uncle was planning on selling the hotel, he had no choice but to come up with a plan. There was too great a risk that any new owner of the hotel would carry out renovations and uncover it. Or worse yet, if it was knocked down, then the treasure could be lost forever. So, he reached out to his daughter, and she agreed to come here and recover the treasure before the hotel was sold.'

'So, it had nothing to do with the release of his cellmate then?' asked Perry.

'No, that was simply coincidence and bad timing. It turns out he had given him a completely bogus location anyway, so he was never worried about him being out and about and finding it. Sabrina Marx also admitted to setting off the explosion in the kitchen. As we thought, it was a distraction, so she could recover the crown jewels from the wall. It was her that locked the door leaving us stranded down in the catacombs and she was able to run about the hotel, completely above suspicion, due to a recording playing on her phone of her exercising in her room.'

'All very clever, but what I don't understand is how she was going to escape afterwards,' said Perry who scratched his tangle of messy hair.

'She, or her father more likely, had thought of everything. It turns out she arrived at the hotel by small boat and that's how she would have left. The police found it later. The weather and lack of a bridge was not going to hinder her. She would just have disappeared as soon as the coast was clear. If their plan had worked, we would be sitting here none the wiser, talking about the mysterious case of the missing guest. All their planning however couldn't account for the chain of events your uncle set off. I'm sure like the rest of us, she believed a killer was stalking the hotel.'

'This sounds so unreal; I can't believe it really happened.' Perry stood up briefly and started to massage his numb buttocks.

'You know Perry, I'm glad your Mum is back, you have picked up some very bad habits in her absence. Now sit down, I'm almost finished.'

'Sorry,' he muttered.

'My mother told me that the Sergeant is going apocalyptic. He has never had so much paperwork to do in his life. He also downloaded a game called 'Bonkers Banana' and she had to break the news to him that it was his fault for the computer virus at the police station. His commander told him to get all unofficial software off the computers or he would be demoted. She also handed in her notice as cleaner, but now has her first new client. She will soon be maintaining all the computers at the police station. A great advert for her new company. So, it's a new beginning for both of us then,' she said, closing the tin foil book.

'I'll drink to that,' said Perry pulling out two bottles of fizzy pop from his coat pockets, and with smiles on their faces, they both toasted their bright futures.

Anyone who had problems keeping up with the complex web of narrative and plot development I weaved, I hope that cleared up any issues you may have had. If not, then I do not know what more to say, aside from give up reading and pick up a Sudoku instead. Only Joking! Seriously, I have more books to write, and I need your support. 🖤 HB

Epilogue

'Hey kids,' came a voice.

'Dad is that you?' Perry shouted back.

'It certainly is,' said his father, who appeared from between the stone lions. 'I was hoping to catch you both. Hi Malaika, how are you doing?'

'I'm fine thanks Mr B.'

'That was a cracking picture in the paper, well done. Now, before I invite you all into the hotel, Malaika can I just ask, has he been toilet trained yet?'

Malaika looked down at Pretzel, who stared back at her as if expecting a glowing report on his behaviour of late. 'Well, I'll admit it's been slow going, but he is getting a little better, so it should be safe enough.'

'Excellent,' he replied, 'and what about Pretzel?'

'Ha-Ha dad, very funny,' said Perry rising to his feet. He turned to Malaika, 'it's been like this non-stop, happiness and laughs, cuddles, and back slaps. Bring back the fake Uncle Hugo I say.'

They all entered through the hotel entrance into reception and followed Perry's father up the stairs to the 1st floor. He walked them both over to the wall where two covered items were hanging.

'It's a little surprise,' he said, 'we can't have Malaika hogging all the fun now can we. Perry, you know the tradition better than anyone. Now that the hotel is ours, I had this done, and for the record it replaces your uncle's.'

With a swirl of his hand and a flick of his wrist he pulled the covering off, revealing a painting of himself.

'Very nice,' smiled Perry impressed.

'Looking good Mr Bumbler,' said Malaika.

'Thank you, I'm glad you liked it. It was a bit of a rush job, but it was worth it. Don't you think it catches my intelligence, my noble chin, I quite like the ceremonial robe I'm wearing, I kept that for myself out of my brother's wardrobe, and then there's the...'

'Dad,' interrupted Perry, 'why is your name not beneath it?' He pointed to the plaque sitting under the painting which was devoid of any writing.

'I've been thinking long and hard about this Perry and I can't be called Hugo, not after everything that has happened, or Erstwhile obviously. No, I have decided, I'm going to change my name. I'm not sure what to yet, but it will be a fresh start.'

'That's a great idea dad. Just promise me that you won't go for anything too crazy though. Something plain and simple like Joe, John, or Frank. These walls are full of Bumblers with the most ridiculous of names. It's time you and I put an end to it.'

'Ssssh...,' whispered Malaika, 'old Ragamuffin Bumbler down there will hear you.'

They both laughed.

They laughed so much that they didn't notice the slight grimace that passed Perry's dad's face.

'I'll certainly take that onboard son. Well, I'm glad you liked the painting though, now why don't you get off and enjoy the day. You both managed to solve the mystery of the High Hill Hotel and I'm sure you'll want to turn your attention to another adventure.'

'Hang on dad, what about that one there,' Perry motioned towards the second covered object.

'Oh, that's nothing really, we had one painted of you as well. Based on a picture obviously, your mum and I wanted it to be a surprise. You'll own this hotel one day.'

'Wow, thanks dad, let's see it then.'

'There's no hurry, plenty time for all that, go, get off and play.'

'Oh, come on dad, I want to see my painting,' and with that he pulled the cloth off.

There was silence.

'Dad, what's that...?'

'It's a good likeness,' said Malaika. 'They did a bang-up job, that mess of hair is so life like, I bet if I was to touch it, I would get my fingers stuck in it.'

'**DAD..**,' said Perry loudly, 'what is that?' he pointed towards the name plaque below the painting.

'Ah, yes, well me and your mum were going to tell you at some point, when you were a little older, but under the circumstances...'

'WHAT... IS... **THAT...?**' demanded Perry.

'It's... it's your name son, your full name. We just called you Perry for short.'

Perry felt completely numb.

'You... you mean to tell me that my name is Periwinkle. **PERIWINKLE!**'

The colour drained from ~~Perry's~~ Periwinkle's face.

Malaika dropped to the floor in a fit of giggles, fizzy pop shooting out of her nose in all directions. Her bellowing laughter filled the building, it flowed down the stairs, flooded through reception, and burst out across the sun kissed grounds of the High Hill Hotel.

Epilogue 2

Two for the price of one...

An extract from one of the letters owned by Mr Gentle-Me.

.... and I threw their flaming and smouldering bags out of the top floor window. They will not be coming back to this hotel again anytime soon.

But how are you Seymour? I certainly hope you are enjoying the French Riviera at this time of year. I am quite jealous.

I had a most excellent game of noughts and crosses yesterday. It is a game that is sweeping the nation and I feel myself very blessed. Erstwhile is of an age, and his birthmark large enough, to provide a tangible benefit in life.

It makes for a fantastic, ready-made template for my friends and I to use. True, we only play the one game a day, but it does have the added benefit of alerting me to the fact if the scoundrel has skipped bath time again...

Epilogue 3

Really!

'I can't wait to see him,' growled the hulking giant as he was led down the grey corridor of the prison. His face an ugly grimace, impossible to tell if he was smiling, due to the long greasy unkempt hair and beard.

'Well, you will get your wish soon,' said the first guard. 'You've barely been gone; we didn't even get a replacement for you. We are walking you straight back to your old familiar cell.'

The Sopwith Strangler then allowed himself a smile. It was worse than the grimace, a frightening affair filled with ugly stained teeth.

'I have to admit, I never had you pegged as a grave robber,' said the second guard. 'Is this a new hobby you picked up? Love a bit of fishing myself, nice and relaxing, tranquil. But grave robbing, I don't see the appeal. All that sneaking around in the dark with a shovel, it's all a bit... strenuous, isn't it?'

The Sopwith Strangler gave another deep throaty growl as he grew agitated. The guards struggled to keep his giant, heavily muscled frame, on course.

'He lied to me,' he hissed. 'I watched his back, all those years and he lied. The treasure was never in that graveyard. He's going to pay for deceiving me. Oh, how he will pay.'

'Enough of that kind of talk,' said the first guard, 'we don't want any trouble on our watch, save it for the morning shift.'

They stopped in front of a pitted and scarred door of heavy iron, painted in the same depressing grey as the walls.

'Home sweet home Billy,' sang the first guard. He banged heavily on the door. 'I hope you're decent in there, we have an old friend who's come for a visit.' He fished out a key and opened the door.

The second guard looked up at the beast of a man. 'We informed Mr Marx earlier today that you were coming. Don't be offended, but he looked less than happy at hearing the news.' Both guards smirked.

'Now, why don't the pair of you just kiss and make up. You'll both be in here together for a long, good while.'

The three of them shuffled into the tight darkened cell. The first guard prodded the sleeping figure on the bed.

'Hey Sinclair, wake up, we have a little present for you. Someone wants to say hello.'

The lump refused to move, which made the guard annoyed, this was messing with their fun.

'Hey,' said the second guard, 'didn't you hear him?' He whipped the covers off the bed. Revealing nothing but a strategically formed lump of pillows.

'He's... he's gone,' he said in a stunned voice. 'He's not here...'

'Raise the alarm,' shouted the first guard down into the corridor. **'The Plimsoll Bandit... he's escaped...'**

Epilogue 4

Okay, this is getting ridiculous...

The Man That Was Erstwhile Bumbler

With less than a year in full charge of the High Hill Hotel, bookings were already through the roof. The excellent reputation of the hotel had travelled far and wide. Under the management of Bombardier Bumbler, as he was now calling himself, it also won several prestigious awards. It was clear this hotelier was destined for great things.

Sabrina Marx

Ms Philippa Harrumph, better known as Sabrina Marx, had repented on her short life of crime, and spent most of her days in the prison kitchen, diligently trying to perfect her Chudge recipe.

Seymour Gentle-Me

Mr Gentle-Me put off his well-deserved retirement and made himself another fortune after developing a range of fashionable anti-strangle cravats.

Grubbins

As yet, no attempt has been made to climb the 'Nubbin', but Grubbins did win the cocktail maker of the year after finally being allowed to play around with some quality ingredients. To date, he has still not trimmed his sideburns.

Belinda

Belinda wrote a best-selling cookbook on how to prepare banquet quality meals under adversity. She has also given several lectures to the S.A.S. (although it was unclear if this was for cooking or unarmed combat).

Jimmy James Jr.

The tall American gave up being a salesperson when his aerodynamic spork failed to ignite the cutlery industry. After brief spells as a hot air balloon pilot and a Tofu inspired rapper called 'J3', he wrote a best-selling mindfulness book called 'What Would the Turtle Do?' Currently his Temple of the Turtle Church is under investigation for being a potential cult.

Sorry Noakes

After a brief stay in a sanatorium, for the dazed and confused, Sorry Noakes and Mr Frock went on to become an internet sensation. They are now successful social media influencers.

Sergeant McSweeney

The Sergeant never fully recovered from the cold he caught that stormy night and the sheer mountains of paperwork that the case brought him. On the cusp of a breakdown, he decided to leave the police force and is now running a successful flower shop called 'Arresting Aromas'. He has also been on several dates with Malaika's mother. Who, for the record, is now running not one, not two, okay it's four, computer repair shops across the country. She has also appeared on the cover of PC Powerhouse as the 'Regent of Repairs'.

The Sopwith Strangler

After having read a popular mindfulness book, the Sopwith Strangler took up yoga, which brought him to a higher plane of peaceful existence. His desire to squeeze things with his hands has now been channelled into pottery and by all accounts he is a natural.

The Plimsoll Bandit

The Bandit has still eluded authorities across the globe and remains at large. He has been linked to a new spate of audacious robberies, not seen since before his incarceration. One of which was suffered by his old prison governor himself, who's collection of rare lace doilies was stolen.

Erstwhile Bumbler

The once upon a time Hugo Bumbler has never truly accepted the drab prison attire forced upon him and has vigorously petitioned for all prisoners to have access to their own wardrobes. That is, of course, if it's okay with his new cell mate, the Sopwith Strangler.

Pretzel

Pretzel is well loved and looked after, and he behaves himself impeccably within the house. That said, when outside, he can still out poo a horse. A fact that vets find terribly baffling.

Periwinkle & Malaika

As for 'Perry' and Malaika, this was the first of their many adventures together, the Horror of the Headless Hatmaker being a particular favourite of mine.

I am Horatio BLOOM and the above is all true, for I have said so.

The End

Acknowledgements

Everyone loves a good lab rat, and I would like to thank my two.

Firstly Mark Sinclair, who proclaimed it was the finest thing he had ever read. He also stated that I had ruined reading for him, as no book could ever compare to this.

Another person who won't be reading for some time is Iain McKay, but only because 'this book made my eyes bleed'. Ah well, you can't please everyone. Get better soon.

I would also like to take this opportunity to thank my other friends and family. Not for your words of encouragement, as there were none, but I will be the bigger person here and thank you none the less...

To Dusty 🖤

Printed in Great Britain
by Amazon